THE UNLUCKY BRIDE

SYLVIA MCDANIEL

VIRTUAL BOOKSELLER, LLC

❀ Created with Vellum

Flood waters and broken hearts...two jilted ex-lovers trapped in Bride, Texas

Laney Baxter's ironic escape to Bride, Texas couldn't be more fitting - considering she is a runaway bride! Unfortunately her plans to hide out have her jumping from the frying pan into the fire when she discovers she is trapped with the one man who broke her heart years ago - Chase Hamilton! Now, she can only hope the rising waters recede just as fast before Chase uncovers the mystery of their past.

Chase returns to Bride, Texas to nurse a broken heart and re-evaluate his life. The family home along the river was supposed to offer him peace and quiet, not the last woman he ever expected to see again. When the river rises, trapping them together, Chase questions whether his heart was really broken or just his ego bruised.

Laney and Chase are forced to face some startling revelations - including the feelings they still have for each other. Can the two work through their tangled emotions before the river recedes, or will long hidden secrets tear them apart?

Bride, Texas books!

Bride and Prejudice by Bonnie R. Paulson
The Unlucky Bride by Sylvia McDaniel
Ticket to Bride by Liz Isaacson
Bride 'em Cowboy by Twist Roberts
Over My Wed Body by Veronica Blade
Sleigh Bride by Neve Cottrell
Bride for Hire by Debra Clopton

PROLOGUE

*1*868
Ellora Shepherd waited, her arms wrapped around her waist as the stagecoach passed her. She'd expected him three days ago. *Him.* Her true love.

The dingy lace hem of her wedding dress fluttered in the afternoon breeze. Rubbing her forehead and ignoring the gritty dust on her skin, she blinked wearily. Would he ever come?

Maybe if they hadn't planned on running away together. Maybe if she had made him stay with her instead of promising to meet her in Texas in a no-horse town that had a bench set up by a natural spring and a post office. That was it. Nothing else.

Well, if he wouldn't come for her, she wasn't going to wait.

She pushed away the biting agony his rejection ripped through her. No, she wouldn't be a victim. Instead, she was going to thrive. And right there, Bride, Texas, was born.

CHAPTER 1

*C*upid, Texas

"Laney Baxter, if you have reservations, back out now," Ally, her best friend and bridesmaid said. "Your son doesn't need a father that badly."

Reaching up, Laney touched the gold heart necklace around her neck. Maybe not, but the boy was growing from toddler to little boy, and her son would do better with the influence of a strong man.

Deliberately, she kept her son's father's identity a secret. No one needed to know, not her family, her friends, or even her best friend. For one thing, it would lead to all kinds of questions she was too embarrassed to explain. Especially to her parents.

"Not really reservations. Roger is just not who I envisioned marrying," Laney admitted, not willing to concede she dreamed of walking down the aisle with Ally's brother Chase.

"Do you love him? Please tell me you are not shackling yourself to a man you don't care about."

"Of course, I love Roger. He's a good man. But I expected I would be more excited about tomorrow," she confessed.

Roger was everything she could want. Patient and kind, he

agreed to wait to consummate their relationship. After the pee stick changed color, she made the decision that until a ring graced her left finger and a license proclaimed her his wife, there would be no sharing her bed. What was that old saying?

Once burned, twice shy.

"Don't you think your lack of excitement is telling?"

Flipping her shoulder length brown hair back, she shook her head. "After being heartbroken by Trenton's dad, the disappearance of Jim, nothing about love excites me anymore. My lack of excitement is my attempt to guard my heart."

After an unplanned pregnancy and an abandoned engagement, when it came to men, caution was best.

Ally tossed back her glass of wine. "In high school, you were always the life of the party. Creating more mischief than any of the other girls we hung with. And yet, here you are the night before your big day holed up with me in The Cupid Love Nest bed and breakfast. Not even a bachelorette night on the town. We should be down at Valentino's bar drinking champagne and being toasted."

With a shrug, she said, "I'm a parent now. My son is my first priority."

The idea of getting drunk wasn't appealing. She only planned on marrying once and a clear head was optimal when she took her vows. What if Trenton became sick or called for her? He didn't need an out of control mother.

"Lord, I never realized how much having a child could change a person."

A laugh came from Laney's lips as she considered how her life had changed since Trenton arrived. At first, she'd been distraught over having a child. Now, Trenton was a blessing. When he grinned and held up his arms, her heart clenched with love for her little man. Forsaking her single lifestyle was easy.

Her only regret was his father.

Barely three years of age, Trenton's birth transformed her world for the better.

"Your mom is keeping him while you two go off on your honeymoon?"

"No honeymoon. We're spending the night in Fort Worth, and Sunday, we'll come back here. Monday, I move into his apartment," she said, thinking how odd it would be to leave her family home.

Living with them for twenty-four years was longer than she planned. After her parents learned of her pregnancy, they encouraged and helped her finish college while watching their grandson.

Because of their generosity, she had her bachelor's degree in elementary education. Leaving Trenton with her mother every day while she attended school, eased her mind that her son was looked after and so very loved.

Now, the time had come to grow up and face her responsibilities with a new husband.

Sipping the last of her bubbly, she thought back to that one night, when minus her panties, she let down her guard.

The superstition of dancing naked around the Cupid statue in the town square said the next person you met should be your true love. The consequences of her jaunt around that piece of rock appeared nine months later with the delivery of her beautiful baby boy.

Shame, his father didn't have the courage to listen to her when she tried to tell him the results of their one night together where even a condom didn't stop her from getting pregnant. Instead, he'd been too busy going off to graduate school than to learn they were expecting.

One day when Trenton was old enough, they would have a long talk about his father. It would be hard to keep the bitterness from her voice and the anger from her words. His father followed his dreams while she had their child.

"If you decide against this wedding, you're welcome to escape to the family cabin on the banks of the Leon River right outside Bride, Texas. That crazy little town started by the jilted bride."

"A jilted bride started that hole in the wall?"

"Yes, she was stood up by her fiancé and she created a life for herself right there. A beautiful story to remind brides that sometimes there is something better coming along," Ally said, smiling. "It's one of the reasons I like it there."

"Thank you, but I won't need a place. I'm getting married in twenty-four hours."

"Well, here's the key to the cabin," Ally said, dangling the metal like a temptation. "I'll carry it in my bouquet, just in case."

Laney giggled. "Thanks, but next week, I'll be moving into Roger's apartment as his wife and he as Trenton's father."

Ally took a deep sigh and released it. "You realize you have the worst luck with guys. What makes you think marriage will be any better?"

"Yes, I agree I'm unlucky when it comes to men," she said, her eyes blinking with unshed tears.

This was her second endeavor at standing before a preacher and saying vows. Not long after the birth of Trenton, she met Jim who asked her to marry him, only six weeks before the ceremony, he walked away. Disappeared without a call, without a trace.

An unplanned pregnancy, a broken engagement, and now the night before her big day, she had jitters. Nothing more than nerves.

Ally shook her head. "Don't know why, I always thought you would wed Chase. Ever since my brother picked you up that night we dared you to dance in the buff around Cupid, I pictured the two of you together."

"Sometimes even Cupid gets it wrong," she said, knowing she thought she would wed him as well.

❦

LANEY STOOD in the vestibule of the church, in her white satin dress and veil waiting for the wedding march to begin. Doubts assailed her like hail in a Texas thunderstorm. Just like Ally had the night before, she questioned if she should marry Roger.

A gorgeous, rock-solid man who had a great job, supported her, treated her special, kissed well...*but not as earth moving like the man who broke your heart*, her conscious reminded her.

Reaching up, she touched the gold heart necklace, still wondering who had sent her the jewelry. Not long after she did the Cupid dance, it arrived in an unmarked box. No return address, no name, nothing. Now, she considered it her lucky charm.

"Are you certain?" her father asked. "It's not too late to back out."

"Let's go, Daddy," she said, refusing to let her apprehension overcome her. "He's a good man."

"Yes, he is," her father replied. "Is he the right man for my daughter?"

"Come on, Dad. They're waiting," she said, plastering a smile on her face, not answering. That would be a long discussion. One they didn't have time for.

"Okay, let's go," he said and patted her on the hand.

Walking down the aisle, she barely glanced at the people who were seated. Her eyes were on the man she was about to commit her life to, hoping she was making the right choice.

As she neared Roger, she noticed he appeared anxious. Sweat beaded on his forehead. Of course, he was nervous. They were making a lifetime commitment today. A major life event.

Smiling, she tried to reassure him as she approached the altar.

"Who gives this woman away?"

"Her mother and I," her father said, handing her off to Roger. Placing her hand in his, she gave a quick, reassuring squeeze.

The pastor looked out at the people gathered for the ceremony. "Should there be anyone who has cause why this couple should not be united in holy matrimony, please say so now."

The door of the church slammed open and the sound of high-heels running down the aisle had her frowning as she watched Roger's eyes widened, his mouth dropped open, and she knew. Like a bolt of lightning, she just knew...

The color faded from her fiancé's face as he gasped, and her stomach tightened. Taking a deep breath, she fortified herself for the bad news. Unlucky again.

"Excuse me, but this man is married," a shrill voice sounded as their friends and family mumbled to each other.

A short woman with bottled-blonde hair and a set of decorated designer boobs displayed down to the top of her nipples, stood waving a piece of paper, a hefty rock on her left hand. "This is a copy of the marriage license. I have a ring on my finger and our wedding photo."

Reaching for her beacon of hope, Laney's fingers flew to the golden heart necklace around her throat.

Relief seemed to flood Laney and the look of horror on Roger's face made her burst out laughing. From the distress etched on his face, she grasped the woman's claim was true. Anger flooded her body like a Texas downpour racing through the streets. The man who supposedly loved her let her make a complete fool of herself.

"You low-life jerk," she said low enough for only his ears. "You're married. When were you going to tell me?"

"No, no," he cried as she walked back down the petal covered carpet, her satin skirt swishing, determination in every step to elude this fiasco.

"The marriage is not real. It happened in Vegas," Roger howled. "Stop, Laney, stop."

"Oh, yes, it did," the woman said. "We met, spent the night together, and woke up the next morning in wedded bliss. After I went to get coffee, you left before we talked about where we're going to live."

"That was fake," he exclaimed.

"Oh no, baby. This sealed document is as real as it gets. You belong to me."

Nearing the heavily made-up woman, Laney sensed her parents surrounding her, her precious son in her mother's arms. The touch of her father's hand at her elbow, guiding her around the circus she could see unfolding there in the church, was comforting.

Roger begged his new wife to stop as she shoved the paper that shackled him to the platinum bombshell in his face. "Honey, I'm so glad I showed up. Bigamy is against the law."

"Right now, jail would be better than the hell I'm living."

The vulgar woman laughed. "That's not what you said in bed the other night."

Hurrying past the unfolding chaos, a loud scuffling noise came from behind. Looking over her shoulder to see Roger sprawled in the aisle, a satisfied look of retaliation spread on her grandmother's face.

Granny could be deadly with her cane, buying Laney time to escape the auditorium. Smiling at the woman she loved, she gave her a thumbs up.

Laney hurried out the chapel. Funny, she wasn't crying. She wasn't even sad. Actually, she felt at peace. As they reached the vestibule, she turned to her mother and took her son from her arms.

"What are you doing?" her mother asked, emerald eyes filled with tears.

"I'm leaving town for a little while," she said, knowing instinctively this was what she should do. Hide out from the drama swirling around her and Roger. Getting away was the only reason she would have any serenity. Moving as swift as her taffeta skirt would allow, she made her way past the stunned wedding planner.

"Let me keep Trenton," her mother said, running after her.

"Thank you, Mom, but I need my son. Give me a chance to get away, and I promise, I'll call you later. At the moment, I must leave."

The impulse to race as fast as she could from the scene of her latest disaster sped through her like the adrenaline of running. The fight or flight urge was all flight. The flaxen-haired sex kitten could have Roger.

In a fog, she entered the bride's room, picked up the overnight bag. Trenton would need more clothes in a few days or a washing machine would work, but she didn't care. Thank goodness, her suitcase was already in the trunk of her car.

Soon as she could grab the rest of her stuff, she would run out the building, though she had no plan where she would go.

Following behind her into the suite, her mother's face was streaked with tears. A distressed frown crinkled her father's fore-head as he tried to comfort her mother while he scrutinized his daughter.

"Mom, I'm all right. Let me slip away so Roger can't reach me. The wedding was ruined by his lovely new wife and I hope they're very unhappy together."

"Your mother stopped me from punching him," her father said. "I wanted to deck him."

"Thank you," she said, her heart aching for the hurt her parents were feeling as she reached over and kissed them each on the cheek. Just then, she heard Roger's voice yelling for her at the top of his lungs.

"Mom, Dad, I'm sorry, I've got to get out of here. Trust me, I'm okay, but I don't want to speak to him."

Reaching into his pocket, her father pulled out a wad of cash.

"In case you need something. Don't forget to call. We'll be waiting to hear from you."

"As soon as we arrive," she said and squeezed her mother's arm.

"Be careful," her mother said and her father wrapped her in his arms.

Picking up her bags, Laney rushed down the hall to the chapel exit, her wedding dress swishing. If only she had time to change clothes. At the door, she saw Ally leaning against the frame, twirling a key.

"Told you so," she said and handed her the shining metal.

"I don't..." The cabin was the perfect place. A small little house tucked on the river, away from town, away from everyone until the melodramatics died down. The kind of place to disappear for a while. Soak up the sun and rest.

"The weather is supposed to become nasty later today, so be watchful. Call me if you have any trouble," Ally said. "Even if you want a little company."

Laney gave her an awkward hug. "This is why I love you. Trenton and I will enjoy the solitude and the quiet."

When the dust settled, she would tell Ally how right she was about her luck with men, but right now, she had to leave or face Roger.

"Now, go. Somehow a reporter showed up and is wanting to do a story on the Unlucky Bride. An interview you don't want to give."

A sarcastic laugh bubbled up from within her. "Why do I have the worst luck when it comes to men?" A glance at her son and her heart swelled with love. "Except that one time I got you, buddy."

"Go," Ally commanded. "And be careful of the—"

Suddenly a flash bulb went off in her face. Ducking her son's head, she ran to her car - all decorated with streamers announcing they were man and wife.

A curse slipped from her lips.

"No, Mommy, bad word," Trenton told her.

"You're right, son. Mommy won't say it again," she promised.

"Where's Roger?" he asked.

"Gone for good," she said and buckled him in his seat.

Starting the car, she drove out of the parking lot, prophylactics flying from her grill, tin cans bouncing behind her, streamers proclaiming just married. More like, publicly dumped.

✿

THUNDER RUMBLED, the house shuddering as Chase Hamilton stared out the window at the rain streaming from the sky. Why in the hell had he come here to this little cabin in the middle of godforsaken nowhere?

Growing up in Cupid, Texas, where people danced naked around a boy in a diaper sculpture to find their true love, he was shocked to learn how a jilted woman started this beautiful community. His parents' weekend getaway sat about a hundred feet from the Leon River, right outside Bride, Texas - where jilted women sought answers to their love life.

What about cheated on men? Where did they go?

To a home along the Leon River to heal. Two broken ribs, a black eye, and a bruised heart. In an irresponsible act of rage, he threw the first punch, creating a scene and barely escaping arrest. All because Cissy, who he enjoyed dating, didn't believe in monogamy. Now, he asked himself, had she been worth all the pain and anger.

Hell, no.

Limping away from the window, he sank back onto the couch, placing the ice pack on his bruised body. Staring at the blank screen of the television, he pondered his life, taking stock of where to go from here.

"Fighting is for losers," he said out loud, his brain agreeing with him. His heart saying *come on, you'd punch the jerk again.*

You don't hit women, children, or animals and the man had done two out of three in front of Chase causing him to lose his meager self-control.

Sadly, Cissy's dramatics outweighed the positives and left him reeling. In the end, she'd chosen the muscled brute over Chase, regardless that the wrestler kicked her dog and slapped her beautiful face.

That kind of crazy, he didn't need - though until then, she seemed so perfect.

Headlights flashed through the darkened room and slowly he rose to his feet. Who could be driving out here in this awful weather? No one knew he had escaped here to lick his wounds and mend in private.

A small Honda splashed on the dirt drive leading to the house. What were they doing coming out here now?

The car stopped and a woman opened the car door and stepped out. Her head bent to avoid the slashing rain drops as she reached inside the backseat of the car. As the woman turned and faced him, his chest tightened, his stomach churned, and he couldn't believe his eyes.

Laney Baxter in a long, lace wedding dress dashed through the puddles running toward the cabin, a little boy in her arms. The memory of their one night together slammed into his gut, wrenching his very soul and he groaned. Not what his recovery needed.

Stepping under the awning, she set the child down and he heard the key in the lock. Chase yanked the door open and she jumped back, her eyes wide with fright.

"Chase," she said in shock, her emerald eyes widening. How he loved gazing into her eyes, feeling like he'd come home.

Shaking his head, he confirmed his eyes weren't betraying him, she was indeed wearing a wedding gown.

"Where's the groom?"

"Left him at church," she said, emptying water out of her shoes.

"What the hell are you doing here? Where did you get a key?"

"Ally told me I could use the cabin for a while."

"Well, she's wrong. You've got to leave."

Laney reached up and ran her hand through her wet hair and glanced down at her son who stared up at her in confusion. "Momma?"

"Ally didn't tell me you would be here. I'm sorry," she said. "I thought I would be alone."

"She doesn't know I'm here. No one knows and I want to keep it that way."

"Little late for that," she said. "When I return, she's going to want to know why."

The little boy tugged on the tulle of her gown and Chase wondered what happened that she came here and not on her fabulous honeymoon.

"Momma," he said a little louder.

How could a man or a woman hit a child or an animal? Yes, he'd been wrong to stoop to the man's level, and yes, he was paying the price for his rage. When his fist connected with the tough wrestler's cheek, the explosion of flesh and bone felt good, until his retaliation shot landed in Chase's ribs.

Never one to wrestle and throw a punch quickly, he had been no match against the professional.

Glancing down at the child, the vision of a screaming toddler invading his personal space made his decision. They had to leave.

"Tell her you couldn't reach the house. Tell her anything. But you can't stay here."

"You're going to send us back out into the storm," she said, her eyes narrowing.

The two of them shared one magical night of being together,

and right now, his heart was dealing with his latest love disaster leaving him vulnerable. Too vulnerable to the charms of Laney. Even in her wet, muddied, now ruined, wedding dress, her mahogany hair falling around her shoulders, she looked stunning.

Whatever happened, the man had been a fool to let her go, and Chase couldn't be around her. Not now, not even with a downpour raging outside. She was hurricane force winds of danger compared to cold front Cissy.

"Momma, I need to go potty," the little boy said impatiently. "Now."

"Can my son at least use your restroom before we go back out into the storm?"

A twinge of guilt gripped him and his logical side reminded him of the dangers.

"Of course," he said. He wasn't a complete monster. Just a man confused and hurt and trying to recover.

Taking the boy by the hand, she led him into the living area and straight to the bathroom. In fewer than five minutes, they returned.

"Come on, son, let's go."

"We're not staying?"

"No, we're not," she said defiantly and walked out the door without saying goodbye. "Men are such dicks."

Peering out at the pouring rain, he watched from the door as she loaded the little boy into the child seat in the back of the car. Regret ate at his insides, he should stop her. The thought of a kid running through the house, making noise and the constant presence of Laney kept his lips shut.

Climbing into the car, she started the vehicle and backed away.

Chase closed the door, the silence eating at him. He should have let her stay. Frustrated, but thinking he'd been heartless, he yanked open the door to stop her. Running into the rain after her, to keep her from going, all he saw were tail lights going down the long drive.

One minute, he was trying to save someone and getting injured in the process, and the next, he was sending a woman and child out in a storm. Maybe she was right. Maybe he was just as much of a dick as Cissy's new love.

CHAPTER 2

*L*aney's hand gripped the steering wheel as the rain continued to gush from the sky. Lightning danced across the heavens and thunder shook the ground. Who sends a woman with a small child out on a stormy night?

With every second, her anger compounded, growing until her body trembled with fury. Twice today, she'd been betrayed. How much more damage could men expect her to accept before she retaliated?

The headlights of her car shimmered across fast moving water, the bridge no longer visible. Her stomach lurched into her throat as she slammed on the brakes, her little car fish-tailing in the slick watery slush. Sliding toward the flood waters, the car finally came to a stop fewer than five yards from the raging river.

Breathing hard, her knees bouncing uncontrollably on the seat, gazing at the flooded roadway was the final straw. The end to a very long bad day. It was all too much. Laying her head on the steering wheel, she was tempted to bang her head against it. Her hands clenched the wheel tightly as she cried. Great heaping sobs came from inside her as she wailed.

With startling clarity, her heart pounding in her chest like a hammer hitting a pin, she realized they could have drowned. Mere seconds kept her from driving them into that swollen floodwater, killing her sweet son.

"Mommy," she heard the voice from the back. "Don't cry. It's okay."

The sob fizzled in her chest and she swiped the tears off her face. Time to pull her big girl panties on and be the mom of that little boy. Time for Chase Hamilton to suck it up. Tonight, he had guests, welcome or not, and she just dared him to stop her.

Nobody provoked a momma bear and now she was more than pissed; she was fighting mad.

"You're right, son. Everything is going to be okay. Starting now."

"We going back?"

"Yes, son, we are. Hold on," she told him as she spun the car around almost getting stuck as her tires revolved crazily in oozing muck.

Trenton laughed. "Do it again, Momma."

"Not unless you want to walk, little guy."

"No, me tired."

"Me, too, son."

Pressing the gas, she drove her little car as quickly as she could on the saturated road back to the house. They had as much of a right to sleep there as he did.

Pulling up to the house, the door opened. Lifting the wrinkled muddied tulle, she crawled out of the automobile once again. The horrid wedding gown now looked like she wore the dress in a mud wrestling competition. Opening the car door, she helped Trenton out.

"I see you're back," Chase said, leaning against the door.

She stopped in front of him, pushed her chest out, ready to do battle. Taking a deep breath, she longed for him to keep her from going inside. Doubling her fists, wanting to punch him if he tried to stop her.

For the first time, she noticed his blackened eyes. One was really dark and the other green from the obvious beating he'd received. Too bad they got to him first.

"We almost died," she said, her voice quivering with outrage. "Flood waters have covered the bridge and there's no way to get out of here. We're staying the night, whether you like it or not. Ally gave me the key and we have every right to be here. So suck it up, buttercup."

He started laughing, which infuriated her, riling the rage that rose inside her like a volcano ready to spew.

"You can stay in the second bedroom. After you left, I felt bad. But I never thought about a flood closing the road."

Laney glared at him, her hands shaking from almost speeding into the rushing water. Whatever makeup remained on her face must look a wreck with her tear streaked complexion, but she didn't care. This man lost the advantage he had over her years ago.

It would be a hot day in Antarctica before she let him back into her life.

"Baby, take your toys and go to the room we're sharing. Mommy will be right in." A frown formed on the boy's face as he glanced between them before his tired little legs took him to the room where she could see him.

Chase didn't even have the decency to help her with her luggage.

Walking back out to the car, she carried in their suitcase, went into their sleeping chamber, and closed the door, effectively shutting him out.

Trenton, bless him, the boy had already fallen asleep on the bed. Staring at the child, her heart wrenched at how close they'd come to death.

Damn Chase.

Sinking down, she covered her face with her hands. After

everything that happened earlier today, she almost killed them tonight.

❧

CHASE WATCHED as she disappeared behind the bedroom door in her soaking wet wedding gown. He'd been a class A jerk. Obviously, the ceremony had not gone off as planned and he was tempted to call his sister and learn the scoop. But then he would have to reveal his reasons for being at the cabin.

After that, the cavalry would descend, and his peace, rest, and relaxation would be history. The time in which he planned to redeem and discover who he was as a man would now be interrupted with the arrival of Laney and her son. Was he still dreaming of a beautiful woman with confidence and money who believed in monogamy?

If so, why did he choose the wrong women? Now, he needed to regroup and consider that Cissy might not be the woman for him.

Going into the kitchen, he remembered that Laney liked hot tea. Maybe a little kindness would ease the tension.

With a clank, he put the kettle on and took out some snacks, wondering if while preparing for her big day, she took time to eat anything. The brew was ready, refreshments on the table when he knocked on her door.

The portal opened a crack, her facial expression, not welcoming or forgiving in the least. "Yes."

"There's hot tea if you'd like some."

A frown drew her forehead together. "With or without arsenic?"

With a laugh, he said, "Without."

"Give me a few minutes and I'll be out."

When she came out, she had showered, her hair damp, face

clean of the ruined makeup and her tear streaks gone. But the chip on her shoulder could be seen from space.

In her arms, the wadded-up wedding dress. "Where's the trash?"

He pointed to the receptacle in the corner and she walked over and crammed the satin and tulle inside.

"Don't you want to save the gown?"

The chill coming from her gaze could freeze water. "What's the point? It's damaged beyond repair."

Already on edge, he didn't want to question her as to what happened. So instead, he handed her a cup. "Are you hungry? I laid out snacks just in case you hadn't eaten."

"No," she said. "Thanks for the tea. Who got to you before I did?"

"Just a little tiff with a man who is dating my girlfriend. Before you arrived, I was here to sulk in private, and I'm sorry I let my hurt and anger cloud my judgement."

"Hope he looks worse than you do."

"No, he was a MMA fighter. I didn't stand a chance."

A snort came from her, but she didn't offer any sympathy. Not that he looked for any. With a hard blow, the man might have killed him, if Cissy hadn't stopped the fight.

"Doesn't look like your big day went too well." The words leaped from between his lips and he longed to call them back.

"No, I thought it would be a great day to go for a drive here all dressed in my finery. Get mud all over the satin and lace and be rejected a second time in one day. You're an asshole. We could have drowned."

A cringe went through him and he knew he deserved whatever crap she dispensed toward him. Years ago, he learned when making a mistake, own up to it.

"You're right," he said, knowing he acted irresponsibly, but desperately wanting the place to himself.

"Driving blindly in the deluge, I didn't see the rushing water until I came up on the bridge. Speeding down the road, the car was going too fast and I slammed on the brakes to keep from going into the river. For a moment, I didn't know if we would stop or slide right into the swift water. My son..."

A sob escaped her and she quickly took a drink.

Great, just great. Now, she would deem him the biggest louse on the planet. "I'm sorry. I wasn't expecting anyone. Let alone you and your kid. Right now, I'm not good company. And the weather," he ran his hand through his hair. "That snuck up on me and I didn't know how bad it was out there."

The look she shot him pierced his soul and should have sent him straight to the underworld where she thought he belonged. "You think I'm good company? How would you feel if some woman stood up before your nuptials were to be said and told all your family and friends that she married your man the weekend before? Then shoved the license in everyone's face to prove she was his legal wife."

Wow, that was as bad if not worse than his dilemma. What if he could extend a promise for remuneration?

"Did your parents pay for today?"

"Of course. The dress, the catering, the cake and flowers. Easily ten grand to see their only daughter, once again unlucky."

"I'll help you recover your costs," he said, thinking his secretary would file suit as soon as possible.

A clap of thunder rattled the house and he thought about what would have happened if she'd driven into the water. Their deaths would have been his fault. One more thing to lay on his conscious.

"What makes you think you're unlucky?"

Again, her eyes wanted to pierce him with daggers and leave him for dead. After taking a gulp of the hot liquid, she set the cup down and stood from the bar stool.

"Thanks," she said and walked down the hall to her room.

For a little bit, he thought things were going better. It almost seemed like they were talking civilly to each other, but something set her off once again.

Getting up, he rinsed out the cups and strolled to the window and looked out at the rain. The wind had eased up, but the torrent continued. Thank goodness, the house sat back at least a football field away from the river.

The image of her little car bobbing in the water caused his gut to clench in a knot. Finding out your woman cheated on you was one thing, but to be responsible for the drowning of a child and his mother would devastate him.

Yes, his solitude had been short-lived. A time when he intended to reflect on his choices in life interrupted by a woman he secretly feared. Laney had been his sister's best friend for as long as he could remember. A smart, beautiful young woman who intrigued him.

And then one night everything changed when she awakened feelings he couldn't handle. So, he ran back to school away from the passion and desire she evoked.

Both of them were hurting and they had no recourse but to share the home. It seemed like she still hadn't forgiven him for that one night of the best sex of his life and he never called her again. That one night made him realize Laney Baxter was dangerous.

❧

SHAKING, Laney closed the bedroom door. Leaning against it, she touched the necklace around her throat. Clenching her teeth, the anger bubbled inside her stomach like she'd eaten bad food, the urge to scream rising from her chest. How in the hell had this happened? She was landlocked in a cabin with the very man who hurt her the first time.

Four years ago, she acted impulsively to a dare by her girlfriends to dance naked around the Cupid statue and she had, until the sheriff arrived. The girls drove off leaving her stranded, exposed, and scared she would be arrested. Only Chase pulled up at the park and yelled at her to get in his car.

And she had. Jumped in without a stitch of clothes on, trying to cover herself with her hands, feeling so foolish and angry at her friends. Like a gentleman, he gave her his jacket and a pair of sweat pants he wore to the gym. Only they hadn't stayed on long.

After getting a soda at the local hangout, they went out to the lake. On a whim, they decided to walk in the woods. When the moon disappeared behind the clouds, they became hopelessly lost. All night, they held each other, trying not to panic, seeking pleasure in the other's arms.

In the moonlight, they evolved into lovers, or so she believed. After talking for hours, they sat shivering, holding onto one another, waiting for the dawn. Before daylight, they managed to find their way back to the car and hurried home. That fateful morning, he kissed her goodbye and said he would call.

She never heard from him again. Six weeks later when the pee stick showed a plus sign, terrified, she sought him out to tell him she was expecting their child.

Only when she arrived at his house, his car was packed, and he was saying bye to his family, headed to law school. Once again, he assured her he would call and like before, her cell phone never rang with his number.

Glancing at her son curled up in the bed, sleeping soundly, a tear rolled down her cheek. A powerful pain gripped her chest filled with more love than she could handle for this kid. How could Chase walk away from this little boy who made her world a happy place when everything else turned sour? But then, again, he didn't know he existed and never would.

"Don't worry, Trenton, I'll take care of you. You'll become a man women adore. Someone who doesn't run from responsibility."

CHAPTER 3

*T*he next morning, he awoke to the aroma of bacon. In the kitchen, he heard giggling and the memory of the night before came back. A groan rattled his chest.

It wasn't that he disliked kids, but didn't know how to act around small children. The oldest in his family, there were a lot of years since his sister had been a baby. Some of his friends had little ones, but they were smaller than Trenton.

Glancing at the clock, he moaned. Only seven in the morning. This was why he didn't want anyone here in the house with him. What was wrong with sleeping in?

Rising from the bed, he glanced out the window. Though the rain slowed, it still fell from the sky in a steady downpour. The front yard was one big puddle and in the distance, he could hear the roar of the river. Never before had the water reached the house, but there was always a first time.

Throwing on clothes, he walked out of the bedroom. Laney stood with her back to him, scrambling eggs.

"Momma, bad man," her son warned.

Turning from the stove, she glared at him.

"Son, it's not nice to call Mr. Hamilton a bad man. Though, part of me agrees with you."

Well, this was certainly a fine way to start the morning, being ganged up on by a small boy and his mother. He refused to let her get to him.

"Good morning," he said cheerfully, wishing he could go back in time and change their first meeting. "I hope you slept well."

"Not really," she said. "Dreams of floating down the swollen river woke me several times. Visions of being in a church, the water surging upwards as I tried to escape."

"Nightmares," he said.

"Coffee is ready and the scrambled eggs are just about done."

"May I join you?" he asked.

The little boy frowned at him, the child's eyes narrowing. Great, now a toddler's remark left him feeling guilty.

"We won't be disturbing you?" she responded saucily.

"No, I'm trying. The day is young, let's not argue. Besides, it smells delicious."

Since they had to share the space, there was no sense in fighting or arguing. That, he could witness every day in court.

"This is your cabin. Of course, you can join us. The food is yours. Not wanting to do my shopping in my wedding dress, I planned on going to the store today."

The image of her rolling a cart down a grocery aisle brought a smile to his lips. "In Bride, Texas, the women would have surrounded you and told you the legend of Ellora Shepherd the jilted bride who created this town. In their eyes, you would be a heroine."

The town was kind of weird in a crazy good way and Chase always enjoyed coming here. Now, the stigma of being left at the altar was stuck to Laney, and yet, a little spiral of happiness tingled up his spine, surprising him. Not because her ceremony was a dismal failure, but rather, she didn't have a band encircling a finger on her left hand.

"At the moment, I don't want to learn about a successful jilted bride. The knowledge that another woman suffered the same humiliation doesn't make me feel better. But Karma, that girl, she has a way of getting even. Roger and Mrs. Fake Body Parts, may they live happily ever after," she said, her voice sugary sweet.

The woman had a mean streak and Chase felt sorry for Roger and Mrs. Fake Body Parts because as an attorney, their union sounded like a travesty. Certainly, they had a future with an attorney sitting across the desk from them.

"Somehow, you haven't convinced me. No jury would believe your testimony, Miss Baxter. The prosecution thinks you lie," he said.

"You're not supposed to lie," Trenton said, looking up from shoveling food into his mouth. The kid had an appetite. "More juice, Momma?"

"Half a glass more, but then you have to switch to water," she told him.

"Okay," he said not happy. "When can I have one of my boxes?"

"Later," she said and handed Chase a plate with eggs and bacon.

Sitting down with her own breakfast, she gazed around the table, and he watched her face tighten, her eyes filling with tears. Ducking her head, she shoved food in her mouth.

A twinge rippled through him, causing him to tense. Last night, she'd been stoic, and he didn't want to see her cry. Still, she must be disappointed and a little embarrassed at what happened yesterday. Without meaning to, he made her life more difficult.

"I'm sorry about your wedding," he said.

Right now, she couldn't see how much of a bullet she dodged. Later, she would realize how fortunate for her that his new wife attended their ceremony. Though she wanted this marriage, she was lucky the disastrous event left her without that albatross Roger around her neck.

A sigh escaped from her lips. "Your sister kept telling me not to marry him. Even my own gut cautioned me, but I didn't listen. As I ran out of the church, Ally gave me the key to the cabin."

"Then you arrived here, and I acted like a jerk."

With a stern mother's glance at her son, before she gave Chase a warning. "Language."

"Sorry," he said. This was one of the things about children he would have to adjust to.

"Bad word," Trenton said. "Momma says don't say bad words."

"That's right, son," she said. "Finish your bacon so you can go play."

"We're going fishing?" Trenton said, his eyes growing large.

"No, the water is not safe for us to be around," she said. "Look outside, there is still a downpour."

Soon as the little boy finished eating, he jumped down from the table. "All done. Gotta find my truck."

"Check the toy bag," she said.

After the child left, she didn't look at Chase, but ate her breakfast.

"Where's his father?" he asked, wondering who the man was that had gotten her pregnant and what happened to him. What kind of man didn't take care of his son?

At her choking, he reached over and patted her on the back. Grabbing her juice, she gulped the liquid. With a plunk, she set the glass down, her brows drew together in a frown staring at him.

"Too busy for a baby," she said in a calm voice. "Things happen for a reason."

"Does he visit him?"

Yes, Chase asked a lot of personal questions, but he wanted to understand. If the creep declined to help her, then as her attorney, Chase would make the bastard pay for not supporting her boy.

"Until recently, I had not seen him since shortly after the night Trenton was conceived."

"Fool," he said. "He's adorable."

No, he hadn't been around many children or babies, but Trenton seemed like a charming boy.

"Most of the time, yes. Sometimes he has moods kind of like his father. Or should I say most men."

So, she was a little bitter toward men, but could you blame her. Not only had Trenton's father left, but now Roger made their wedding a fiasco.

"Does his father pay his child support?"

She laughed. "We don't count on his father for anything."

Licking her lips, she faced him. "You've made it clear you don't want us here and just as soon as the river recedes and I can cross the bridge, I'll leave."

"You can stay as long as you want, but for now, I'm more concerned about the water reaching the house. If you looked out the window this morning, not only is the river overflowing its banks, but halfway across the yard. And the rain continues to fall. This adventure could end with us leaving in a boat."

Standing from her chair, she started putting the dishes in the dishwasher and cleaning up.

"Where are the life jackets?"

"In the shed, I think," he said.

"Then I suggest you find them before we need them," she said.

With a nod. "You're right. Yesterday, I behaved like an ass. Again, I'm sorry."

The woman clutched her anger to her chest, refusing to turn it loose and begin to heal. He'd apologized several times and if she didn't forgive him this time, he was done asking for forgiveness.

"Let's just make the best of our time together," she said and turned away from him.

Why did he know it wouldn't matter what he said, she would still be angry at him, at men, maybe the whole human race?

ﻻ

WHAT HAD she done to the universe to deserve to be humiliated at her wedding, then stranded in a cabin with the father of her son? Who in his stupidity, didn't know Trenton was his.

Sitting at the table this morning, seeing them all together like a family, she just about lost it. Then when he started asking questions, she wanted to jump up, grab Trenton and run out the door. Unfortunately, she was stuck.

The river made leaving impossible. They couldn't reach medical help or go to the store. Completely cut off from the world, even her cell phone coverage was going in and out.

Honestly, she didn't believe Ally knew her brother was going to be here or she would have warned Laney. But Ally had admitted to believing he should marry her.

Regardless, she had to keep it together or Chase would realize that Trenton was his son. Somehow, she couldn't let her anger at him cloud her judgement and come out in a torrent of disgust. Yet, she wondered why he didn't notice her son had the same cheekbones, the same nose and mouth. A mini replica of himself.

And the questions. The urge to shout *are you so stupid that you don't comprehend he was born nine months after we spent the night in the woods* almost overwhelmed her.

Plugging in her curling iron, the lights suddenly went out, the house shadowed in darkness, that eerie dead silence filling the home. Running into the living room, she found Trenton sound asleep on the floor, his truck lay not far from him. Poor little guy, his schedule was all messed up and the stress of the last few days must have caught up with him.

Picking him up, she carried him into the bedroom and laid him on the bed, closing the door partly. In a strange house, she didn't want him to wake up and be afraid.

As she returned to the main room, she saw Chase putting on a raincoat. "I'm going out to make sure there are no downed power lines and check the breaker box."

A quick glance out the window confirmed the flood waters were no longer climbing. "The river doesn't seem to be getting closer. Be careful."

A grin spread across his face, like this was her lucky day. "Worried about me?"

"Don't get excited. That's something I would say to anyone going out in this weather."

"Oh," he said and shrugged. "I thought we progressed past our truce."

"Nope, we're still at the treaty table, nothing set in stone. Have a great stroll in the rain."

Opening the door, she stared out at the steady water dripping from the sky. A soft drizzle still came down and the bridge was invisible. Unless her car turned into a boat, she would be staying right here.

Thunder rumbled in the distance.

"Bring back the life jackets," she said.

Closing the door behind him, she found a flashlight and lit candles.

An hour passed and no sign of Chase. The skies had grown quiet, though the drizzle still trickled like a water faucet left on. Could something have happened to him? Anxious, she checked on Trenton who was still sleeping. Leaving him unattended in the house, she had to hurry.

Pulling on a raincoat she located in a closet, she hurried outside and gingerly stepped through the puddles to the garage in back. The door was open.

Stepping into the gloom, she saw Chase stood gazing at the electrical box. Immediately, she realized the problem, the man didn't know which lever to pull.

"When you didn't come back, I feared something bad happened," she said.

"No. Found the life jackets and Grandpa's fishing boat. Now I'm trying to figure out this panel."

"Oh, good grief," she said and reached over and flipped the main switch. "We blew a breaker. Now we understand we can't run the dishwasher, the hair dryer, and my curling iron at the same time. Something is going to need to wait."

Halting, he glared at her in the semi-darkness. "Yesterday, I felt sorry for you."

"Oh, so that's why you sent me back out in the storm."

"No, we'd both had harrying experiences with love and I sympathized for you. Not any longer. Now, Miss Smarty Pants, I don't care what's happened to you."

"Good. Maybe I'll make your right eye match your left."

"You can't let that go, can you?"

"Why should I? It bothers you when I mention it."

"Does it bother you when I comment you were outwitted by a fake blonde?"

"For one, how do you know she used peroxide, and two, Mrs. Fake Breasts didn't outwit me. Because of Roger's cheating, I was the victim of her outwitting my spineless fiancé. He's the one who will suffer and rightly so."

"This morning at breakfast, you called her Mrs. Fake Body Parts, thus peroxide hair."

Well, darn, he was partially right.

Okay, a lot happened since her rant earlier. At this moment, she pretty much loathed the entire male population. Being jilted at church made for a bitter young woman. Then again, more than once, she had a fiancé get cold feet. Now being around the man who left her behind pregnant didn't leave her all warm and cozy inside either.

"Definitely fake breasts, but the hair is not confirmed. Though, it certainly appeared to come from a bottle. Exactly, the type of woman he deserves."

"You must really hate men."

"Currently, I'm not a huge fan, but I don't hate anyone," she said glancing toward the house. Didn't she merit some time to be disgusted with her circumstances? "My son is in the house asleep."

Walking out, determined to return to the house where Trenton slept, she moved quickly, sensing the urge to return. Candles burned in the house, she needed to return to the boy.

"If you weren't a man hater, you wouldn't run."

Turning she gave him her best glare. Why was he antagonizing her? If he kept poking the bear, she would come out growling. "Excuse me, I have more important things waiting on me than to stand here in a downpour and argue with you over trivial junk."

Strolling beside her, he continued baiting her. "There's a chip on your shoulder."

"Oh, give me a break. Don't you think I can justify a boulder resting there? After all, I'm the bride who ran out of the service, humiliated. I'm the woman who was left..."

Her mouth clamped down, as terror seized her. The words almost glided past her tongue about how he left her. The silly man didn't even grasp what he'd done.

Before she could tell him she was expecting his child, he climbed in his car and drove off with her standing in the street. Driving off before she had a chance to tell him they had a baby coming in seven months.

Arguing was a waste of her time and her energy. Taking a step, her shoes slipped on the slick mud. He reached out to grab and balance her, and instead, the two of them went sliding. Flailing their arms as their legs came up to meet them and they both landed in a puddle.

A tremor of fury tightened her chest as she gasped. "You pulled me down."

"I did not," he said. "I was trying to help you."

Gazing down, she saw wet, ugly brown splatters covered her clothes as the wetness seeped into her jeans.

His eyes swept over her and he started laughing.

"What?"

"You have mud on your face," he said, grinning.

Without thinking, she scooped up some wet clay and flung it at him. "So do you."

"Hey, that wasn't nice."

"Being nice is an overrated quality. What good has it done me? Men are all jerks."

"Trenton's mommy told him to be nice," he responded and threw mud back at her.

"Oh," she said when the cold slimy stuff hit her chest. "Well, Trenton's mommy has temporarily left the building. Right now, she doesn't want to play nice. She wants revenge."

Fighting, Chase released frustration that had been amplifying for days. For the first time, she could release the tension that had ridden her like a bull coming out of the gate.

Hurling a handful of mud at him dispatched blood rushing through her body, giving her a charge. He retaliated, but this time the clay clung to her chest. He jumped on top of her, pushing her to the ground, pinning her hands. Squirming beneath him, she managed to pull him over, until he lay in the sludge.

Now they were both strewn with the grainy muck from head to toe. As she sat on him, he held her arms. Rolling her again, she found herself on bottom, but this time her strength ebbed, too worn out to fight him off.

"Maybe, you need someone to remind you how, with the right man, it can be great between a man and a woman."

In horror, she watched as his lips descended. Like lightning struck her, she was jerked back to the past, to that night when nothing mattered but the feel of Chase's arms around her. The touch of his skin against her own. The rasping of their breaths mingling as they learned about love and created a child together.

This time, as an adult, she knew the consequences.

Thrusting him back, gasping for air in her chest, she cried, "Stop, I can't do this with you. My son is in the house. I've got to get back inside."

Before she rose, a tickle of awareness hit the back of her neck. Whipping around, she gasped. Standing in the doorway of the house stood Trenton.

"Mommy?"

"Nooooo" Laney screamed as she spied her boy running as fast as his little legs could go and jumping into the mire right in the middle of Chase.

&.

UNPREPARED for the forty pounds of toddler that landed on him, attacking him, Chase took the blow to his midsection. His ribs screamed with displeasure.

"Don't hurt my mommy," the little boy cried as he pummeled his chest with his fists. "Bad man."

"Trenton, stop," she shrieked, pulling him off Chase. "Baby, I'm all right. We slipped and fell in the mud and Chase was trying to help mommy up."

It wasn't the complete truth, but better than if she admitted to fighting with Chase. A quiver of guilt went through him at the realization that the boy walked outside and witnessed the two of them wrestling in the muck.

"You're okay?" her son asked her, looking up, his big brown eyes wide. Those eyes were so beautiful and familiar, yet Chase didn't know why.

"I'm dirty, but fine," she said

"Hey, guy, I thought we were becoming friends," Chase said. "I would never harm your mother."

The little boy looked at Chase but he could tell he had not earned the child's trust. Turning his back on Chase the kid focused on his mother. Looking at her, he giggled. "Mommy, you have mud on your face."

"Well, you should see yourself. It's in your hair and on your shirt," she said and ran her finger down his face. "And now, on your face."

The child's giggles were followed by a loud clap of thunder that announced a new round of storms.

"Let's get inside," Chase said, rising from the puddle where he stared with fascination at the interaction between a mother and her son. This must be how it felt when having a family. The urge to protect them from danger, surged, though he didn't like that the boy believed he would harm his mother or that he was a bad man.

Building trust with the boy would have to be a priority.

Reaching the covered porch, he pulled his polo over his head and reached for his pants not thinking about how it would appear.

"Wait," Laney said. "Don't disrobe here in front of us."

"Well, we can't go inside caked in mud."

Honestly, he hadn't given it much thought, but just started undressing, ready to shuck his wet, muddy clothes.

Halting his movements, he watched her assess the two of them and sighed. "Agreed."

"Turn your back and we'll strip down to our underwear. Leave your clothes out here and I'll put them in the washer."

The child laughed and begin to remove his pants, eagerly shedding his clothing before Chase moved. The kid was funny. A second later, he heard her scold him. "Keep your underwear on. Now, in the house."

Out of the corner of his eye, Chase glimpsed the boy dash into the rain, naked. Stomping in muddy, sludge, he laughed with sheer joy. Oh, to be so carefree again. Lifting his face to the sky, he stuck his tongue out and tasted the falling water drops.

"Trenton, come back here," she demanded.

"Momma, fun," he called.

Chase ran into the drizzle and stomped in the watery muck with him and turned his face to the heavens. Mimicking the actions of the boy, the child stared at him suspiciously and then giggled.

A streak of lightning had him scooping the boy up in his arms and hurrying back under the awning.

"Come on, kiddo. Play time is over," Laney said. "In the house to the shower."

Glancing up at Chase, Laney said, "Thank you."

"This was kind of amusing. Even the mud wrestling. But the part I really enjoyed was the kiss."

The feel of her lips against his reawakened all the desire and passion they created in the past, overwhelming him with how much he'd wanted her that night so long ago.

She frowned. "Before you get any ideas, I'm a jilted bride. There is no way I'm having a rebound romance with you. We've done that once. Not happening again. Now turn your back so I can undress."

Frowning, he stopped. Memories of her Cupid dance and how he had picked her up and taken her to Make Out Lane. Walking around the lake, they took a wrong path in the dark and had gotten lost. Unable to find their way back to the car, they spent the night, waiting for the dawn.

Comforting her and keeping her warm, led to kissing and hunger and eventually sex. That night he had been her first and according to legend, because he was the first person she saw after dancing in the buff, he was her true love.

"Maybe the reason your other relationships aren't working is because we're supposed to be together."

In a swift motion, her head swung around and she stared at him, her emerald eyes large in her pale face.

"Something to ponder while you take your shower," he said and turned back around.

With a plop, the sound of her soaked clothing hitting the ground and his imagination went wild.

"Nothing to ponder, Chase. That was a long time ago and we're no longer college kids. The Cupid superstition isn't real."

The door opened and she was gone. Whirling around, he caught a glimpse of her bare backside going through the house.

CHAPTER 4

Chase walked out of his bedroom, his hair wet from his recent shower. The most incredible urge to lean in close and breathe in his manly scent overcame her and she resisted. Something was happening between them, and this attraction needed to stop. That road they traveled once before and there was no going back.

Too much water over the bridge for her to return to the time when alone and pregnant, he left her to attend law school. No, he didn't know about the unplanned pregnancy, but he obviously had no interest when he drove off and never called.

"Hey, Trenton," he said, sitting next to him at the table.

"Hey," he said back, swinging his legs as he ate his sandwich. "What happened to your eye? It's a funny color."

"Trenton, we don't ask about a person's looks."

"Why?" her son asked, looking up at her.

How could she tell him in terms he would understand? "We don't ask questions about how people look."

Chase leaned over to the child and whispered, "My girlfriend's new boyfriend gave me a black eye and broke two of my ribs."

Shocked, Laney stared at him. She'd known he was in a fight, but not the reason. Curious, she really wanted to hear more, but declined to ask. Masking her face, she refused to let him see she was intrigued.

"Did you hit him back?" her son asked.

Raising a son, she was quickly learning little boy's toughness began at an early age. Trenton was all boy and let her know every day he was male.

"Yes," Chase said. "And I lost the fight, the girl, and I'm injured."

So, the brawl had been over a girl. Both of them were here, two rejected souls looking for some place to lick their wounds and heal their broken hearts.

Glancing at Trenton, the boy's eyes widened and he stared intently at Chase. "What have I told you about fighting?"

"No hit," her son said, hanging his head.

"Last year, he got in trouble at play school," she told Chase.

"Did you win?" Chase asked Trenton and she gave him a thunderous look. You never encouraged a child to take out their frustrations on another.

"No," Trenton said. "Teacher got mad. Did you get in trouble?"

Chase gave a snort. "The worst kind. Lost my girlfriend."

The boy stopped and considered this last comment. "Did it hurt?"

"So much, it reminded me why I don't fight with my fists, but rather words. I knew better, but sometimes injustice gets to me and I acted on my feelings and not my logic."

A smart kid, Trenton would still never understand what Chase just said. But hopefully, they impressed on him enough to learn that hitting another person did not settle disagreements.

"Hurting someone is never a way to solve problems," she said, continuing to make her sandwich.

"What are you eating?"

"Ham," Trenton yelled out. "And chips."

"I'll pay you for the groceries," she said, looking sheepish. "I'd planned on going to the store the next morning, and instead, here we are stuck. How long will it take before the bridge is open?"

With this smoldering temptation between the two of them, she needed to leave at the first available window. When the car could cross safely, she was out of here.

"Has to stop raining first, and no, you're not paying me anything. I'm hoping we don't run out of food before the water recedes. The pizza delivery guy probably wouldn't swim across the river, even for a big tip."

"Pizza," Trenton cried. "I want pizza."

"When we get home, we'll order take out," she promised the child.

"Pepperoni is my favorite," Chase said to her son. "What's your favorite kind?"

"Cheese," he replied enthusiastically.

"Hmmm...with lots of sauce." Chase laughed at the boy. "And gooey topping."

"Hmmm..." Trenton mimicked.

Staring between the two of them, she realized they were bonding. In Trenton's eyes, Chase had gone from that bad man to a pal. Somehow Chase won over her son and the two sat together at the table laughing like good friends. Sharing stories while she tried to be the parent, his father had the role of friend and buddy.

Reaching up, she touched the gold heart necklace at her throat, feeling it's reassurance.

Not fair. Just not fair. She had all the responsibilities while he couldn't even recognize the features on her son matched the ones on his face.

&

LATER THAT EVENING, Chase walked out the door carrying two glasses of wine to find Laney sitting outside on the covered patio.

"Nice night," he said, handing her a glass. "Where's Trenton?"

"Thank you, asleep," she said. "Early to bed and early to rise, that's my son."

Great, that would give him some alone time with Trenton's mother. The boy and he were getting closer, but Laney still had a wall around her, keeping him out. Did he really want in or did he want to return to the brief explosive night they shared in the past? Years ago, they had been good friends, but having sex ended their friendship. At the time, he realized if anyone could keep him from his goals of becoming a lawyer, Laney had the ability to end his dreams.

Even now he was deeply attracted to her, though she was different. Motherhood had changed her. Made her more protective of those she loved.

The sound of bullfrogs drifted in the breeze from the creek.

"It's stopped raining," he said, realizing the water dripping was runoff.

"Yes. Look, you can see some stars peeking through the clouds."

"Soon, we'll be a part of civilization again," he said.

Glancing at him, she sighed. "I owe you an apology for the way I acted when we arrived. That day is a fog of despair and ugliness. Desperately, I needed some time away from everyone, and though I would have preferred it without the bridge being closed, being off the grid has been nice."

Warmth spread through Chase at her words. Since the night she appeared, he'd apologized until he was blue in the face. The fight today seemed to have eased the tension between them. Or maybe the rage had morphed when they kissed into a simmering sexual awareness.

"No apology needed. My actions were a little on the donkey side, when you arrived. Not expecting anyone, I was hurting pretty bad myself. No one knew where I was and suddenly I'm joined by a woman and her son."

Hiding from those in Dallas necessitated being somewhere no one could find him to lick his wounds in private. Today started out tense, but became entertaining and tempting.

"Thanks for sharing your food and your house with us. As soon as the water recedes, we'll leave and you can return to hiding out."

Being alone didn't seem quite as exciting as it once had. In fact, he enjoyed the two of them. Trenton, because he was protective and caring and curious about everything. Laney brought back all the memories of the two of them wrapped together, cuddling to stay warm and calm and creating a bond he still feared.

"Your eye seems to be more green. How are your ribs? When Trenton jumped on you, I cringed inside."

"So, did I." Trying to appear casual about the blow, yet knowing it had hurt like the devil, he shrugged. "The body is healing slowly. The mind...now, I'm more confused than ever. At first, I didn't want her, then I did want her and now...I don't know."

Shaking his head, he took a sip of wine. "She said monogamy was boring. Sure, I understand women cheat, but I thought only men made such moronic statements. Men use that comment quite a bit on the stand to explain their actions. In the court room, it sounds stupid and even more so coming from her lips."

When Cissy said the words, all the divorce cases he'd heard where men tried to justify their action came roaring back. Sorry, it didn't matter who said them, in a relationship three or more were a crowd.

A smile flitted across her face. "In my world, there is only monogamy. Anything else has me calling you and dividing our assets."

"Exactly," he said, glad to know she believed in the institution of marriage and forever.

"Did her boyfriend start the fight?" she asked quietly.

"Oh, no. I had to jump in with both fists and pummel a man who outweighed me and made his living as a professional wrestler. If she hadn't stopped him, I probably wouldn't be here today, but I feel like my man card was yanked."

Tossing back her dark hair, she stared at him. "You're a lawyer, not a fighter. Even if she cheated on you, what made you decide to punch the guy. You use your brain not your fists."

Everything she said was true, but in that moment, his anger had overruled his brain. Especially when the fighter's palm whacked Cissy's face, all his law school training flew out the window and the Neanderthal in him responded.

"Life is simple, don't hit women, children, or dogs and he did two. First, he kicked her dog and sent him flying and then he slapped her. At that point, I lost it," he said, his emotions reliving that split-second decision, ready to jump up and fight again. "In the end, he got the girl. She said to me, 'He's so exciting and volatile. I need to play with him for a little while.'"

Chase tried to mimic her voice, but sounded more like Lucy with a head cold.

Laney started laughing, which brought out all his insecurities. Finally, she held up her hand.

"I'm not laughing at you. It strikes me as funny a modern woman thinks a man who slaps her is exciting. Kick the dog? Oh hell, no. Not if you want to be my friend. And don't think about touching my child unless you want your life seriously cut short."

Smiling at her fieriness, he loved her response and relieved she didn't think he was stupid. "As your attorney, I would recommend you not threaten ill will on another human being."

"Touch my child and you'll be the first person I call to hide the body," she said, her tone exacting. "Trenton is precious and until he's a grown man, he's my responsibility."

The sounds of crickets and the buzz of insects swarming the tiki torches washed over him, soothing and ordinary and normal.

"All I can say is I respect what you did, but she needs counseling. How serious were you about this girl?"

He laughed. That was the problem. Until two days ago, he convinced himself Cissy might be the one. Enough so, he contemplated a future with her. Eventually he might have offered her a ring. Then typhoon Laney arrived, and his world had tilted sideways, sending Cissy into past tense.

"We dated for four months. She's the daughter of one of the partners at the biggest law firms in the city and before I ever met her, I hoped to get on there," he admitted.

"So, you went out with her trying to get in the door," she said, her brows drawing together in a frown.

"No, it was a month before I learned the identity of her father. After we'd been together for a while, I anticipated marrying her. Hopefully, I would be given the opportunity to work for her father. Now, I know that will never happen. Because I'm a one-woman kind of guy."

In today's world, he was considered a dinosaur. Sure, his happily married friends, as far as he knew, didn't cheat, but he also didn't question them about their sex lives. If they were into ménage or multiple partners, he would be disappointed, but that was their business.

"You're prehistoric." The comment made his head jerk. Their thinking was on the same page, but he would never admit that to her without sending her running.

"We're both here because of a loss of a relationship," he acknowledged. Raising his wine glass, he gazed at her. "To better luck next time."

"Amen to that," she said clinking her glass against his.

"The one thing I miss about having a steady girlfriend is the companionship. Until I spent a couple days here alone, I didn't realize how lonely the quiet became. What do you miss?"

The days before Laney arrived were filled with soul searching, trying to decode where he went wrong. Now the reality that

Cissy and he weren't compatible and fit together like a square peg in a round hole seemed obvious. Could he have been forcing his ideals of what he wanted and not facing the actuality of what he needed?

Laney's brow crinkled in thought. "Sadly, I haven't missed Roger. In fact, in so many ways, I believe I received a reprieve. Why would I marry this guy if my only emotion is relief?"

"Seems obvious. You wanted to spend time at the cabin with me."

Sitting out here talking like this, he felt as if he found his long-lost friend. Conversing with Laney was easy and relaxing and an ease settled between them that he couldn't remember feeling in a long time.

A relaxed laugh rumbled from her. "Yeah, right. Ally didn't tell me you were here. Besides, you turned me away, back into the storm."

"No excuse. I was a dick," he admitted. "Yet, I've enjoyed spending time with you and your son. You've made it so less boring."

Reaching over, he grabbed her hand not holding the wine glass, squeezing it, letting the trickle of warmth spread through him. "Here, we are, just a couple of relationship rejects, huddled together in a storm."

"Which is about over."

"Sunny days ahead. Maybe I'll teach Trenton how to fish."

"Or we'll head back to Cupid."

What could he say besides, he didn't want her to leave. Just when they started having fun, she was talking about taking off. He longed to explore the past and discern if any of the passion they experienced in the woods still lingered between them.

"We've got at least one more day, if not two, together. Let's see how things go."

Taking a sip of wine, she looked at him over the glass. "Just as long as there is no romantic involvement."

Hiding behind his wineglass, he tried to obscure his reaction as he stared into her gaze. No, he wanted to explore the feelings that kiss evoked this afternoon, not run and hide from the passion between them.

Obviously, she wasn't ready to accept the growing, simmering attraction. "A couple of rejects like us. A rebound romance is not an option. Not happening."

The memory of their wet bodies snug against one another overcame him, and even in the twilight, her full lips beckoned and he wanted to sample them again, but had the sense to know to wait. Now was not the time to pursue a romantic involvement. Not yet.

Though, Laney was definitely a tempting morsel, if he could, he would love another taste.

❦

SUDDENLY HER PHONE lit up like a Christmas tree, saying she had twelve voicemails from Roger and one from her parents.

"Looks like the cell phone is back in service," she said.

"Great. That means tomorrow I'll be on the phone with the office," he said with a sigh. "It's been nice not having to deal with them."

"This has been lovely, but I think I'll go listen to Roger's messages and call my parents," she said, getting out of her chair. She drained her glass of wine and went inside.

After hearing how Chase became hurt, she wanted to stay mad, she really did. But listening to his reasons made it hard and the kiss they shared earlier in the day reignited all the memories of their fleeting moment together. The one that created her son.

Still, the pain and anger at how he rushed off when she tried to tell him about her pregnancy was a festering wound in her soul. Sure, she understood he had to return to school, but the need to tell him she was pregnant and ask him what he thought they should do seemed only fair. Already, she knew she would have the baby whether he married her or not.

Instead, he jumped in his car and had taken off like a rocket. Like he feared what she had to say.

Glancing at her son, who lay curled on his side in the bed, she couldn't imagine her life without him. Now she worried if Chase ever learned Trenton was his son, he would do everything in his power to take him from her. He had the knowledge, the skill, the ability to sway the court that he could take care of him better than her, though she didn't believe it for a minute.

Regardless, she knew no way would she relinquish her baby to anyone willingly. They would have to pry him from her cold dead hands, and even then, she would haunt them from the grave.

Pushing the button on her phone, she braced herself for the sound of Roger's voice. Sitting in the dark, she started off feeling sad for him that the relationship ended so badly. By the time he finished, she wondered why she ever considered marrying the jerk.

One moment, he was begging her to forgive him and promising her he didn't know. Then he promised her he would get the marriage annulled. Finally, he grew angry when she didn't respond to his phone calls. The last call, he cursed her to the moon and back. Told her he and Betty were on their way to Vegas and he hoped like hell he never saw her again.

The parting shot was if she'd just slept with him, this would've never happened. It was all her fault for not having sex with him.

That one made her laugh out loud. So because she didn't give him what he wanted, he'd found it in Vegas with Betty. Well, great. Happy honeymoon, loser.

CHAPTER 5

nable to sleep, Chase tossed and turned most of the night thinking about Laney and Trenton. Memories from the past flooded him. That night, he remembered giving her his gym clothes to wear and them going to the lake.

It was the summer after he graduated college and he'd been accepted into law school. She just completed her first year of college, and would soon return for her second.

Whoever was Trenton's father, she met him before the fall and he tried to remember if Ally had mentioned anyone. Sometime after she did the Cupid dance around the fountain. Before dawn he made the decision to help Laney. Obviously, Trenton's father was not paying child support and should be. As a lawyer, he had access to public records and locating people.

Picking up the phone, he called his secretary. "Good morning, Brie."

"For someone on leave, you're up early."

"Couldn't sleep," he said, not admitting to the reasons for insomnia.

"Are you feeling better?"

His office had been appalled at what happened and rightly so. One of the partners gave him a stern lecture, telling him not to get into trouble or risk expulsion. A fancy term for fired.

"I'm sore, but the eye is now green, not black. How are things there?"

Two pending cases he was working on, his paralegal watched the evidence trail while they were waiting on results.

"Quiet."

"Great," he said. At least, now was a good time to be out of the office. "Since you're not all that busy, could you pull a birth certificate for me? The name is Trenton Baxter. After you have the certificate, then I want you to locate the man who is the father. We're going to make him pay child support."

"Will do, boss," she said. "Anything else?"

"That's all for now," he said.

"Are you getting lots of rest?" she asked.

The image of Trenton came to mind, jumping on him in the rain, Chase protecting his ribs, in the nick of time.

"Not really," he said. "But I'm getting stronger every day."

"Excellent," she responded. "Oh, by the way, your phone has been melting with hot, sexual voicemails from Cissy. Seems she's made a mistake and wants to make it up to you in the most sensual way."

Brie, his paralegal, listened to his office phone messages and more than once he told Cissy not to leave sexy voicemails unless she wanted her to hear them.

"What did she say?" he asked, remembering how he blocked her number on his cell phone.

A little snort came through the phone. "She's ready to kiss and make up and described how she would show you she was sorry. Way more information than I needed."

Chase sighed. "I'm sorry you had to listen to that. It will be a cold summer day in Death Valley before I date her again."

A chuckle sounded. "Boss, that girl has some nerve."

"More nerve than I'm willing to experience in my life-time. Call me when you learn who the father is listed as on the birth certificate. I want to nail that bastard."

❧

LANEY WOKE up with Trenton in her face, her head pound-ing. "Mommy, wake up, I'm hungry."

The stress of the last few days, the tension, her hormones, the wine from the night before, all compounded into one raging migraine. The urge to roll over and tell Trenton to fend for himself was strong. Fortunately, her motherly sense of duty refused to let a three-year-old fix his own breakfast.

Crawling out of bed, she sat on the edge as nausea rolled through her. Trenton tugged on her hand. "Momma G gives me fruity cereal. I want Momma G's."

How early children learned to manipulate you. She knew her mother didn't give him that brand, but somewhere he'd had a taste and wanted more.

"We're out," she said. "Eat some crunchy rice with me."

"No," he wailed. "I don't want crunchy rice. I want fruity."

Just what her pounding head didn't need. A grumpy little boy who was well on his way to a full-blown tantrum all because they were out of the cereal he wanted.

Taking him by the arms, she kneeled in front of him. "None of that cereal is in the house. The river is over the bridge and I can't get to the grocery store. Your choices are crunchy rice or you go hungry. Do you understand? Momma is not feeling good, so please behave."

His brown eyes stared at her frown, pulling his fat little cheeks into a pout.

"Will you buy me fruities when we go to the store?"

Oh, the kid was blackmailing her and he was only three.

"Do you want breakfast or not? Because if you don't, I'm going back to bed."

"Hungry," he demanded.

"Shh! You'll wake Chase. Give me a moment," she said, rising and looking for her robe. Tightening the belt around her waist, she opened the door and peeked out. The sun slowly rose in the east, and for the first time in days, they were actually going to see a sunrise.

Going into the kitchen, she switched on the coffee, found the cereal and poured milk on the high fiber flakes.

"Nanner?" he asked.

"Sorry, they're all gone," she said. "Hopefully, we'll be able to go shopping tomorrow."

The little boy sighed, but when she set the bowl in front of him, he eagerly began eating.

Preparing her coffee, she couldn't wait to sit and lean her head back. Anything to close her eyes and the throbbing to ease. After fixing her cup, she took a couple of aspirin and then sat on the couch, wishing someone would cut her head off. That way her stomach would settle down and the palpitating would cease.

"Mommy," Trenton yelled.

The hammer inside her skull picked up speed with the echo of his words. "Trenton, shh! No yelling, Chase is still asleep. What do you need?"

"Can I have more crunchy?"

Yes, the sugar was more than he needed, but he was eating, and right now, she had to have time for the aspirin to start working.

"Only if you'll be quiet. You're going to wake Chase."

"But I want him awake," he said in a whiney voice no mother liked hearing, "so we can play."

Freezing, she stared at her son. "What did you just say?"

"Want Chase up, to play," he said.

Two days ago, he called Chase a bad man. Now, they were friends?

"You said you didn't like Chase," she said.

The little boy shrugged and began to dig into his cereal. "He's okay."

The door to Chase's room opened and he walked out in his pajama bottoms minus his shirt. Hard rippled abs with a light dusting of hair across his chest greeted her, making her breathless. Glancing at the two of them, he rubbed his face.

"What are you doing up?"

"Chase," Trenton said and smiled. "Wanna go outside and play?"

"Good morning, sport. The sun is barely up. Don't you think it's a little early?"

"Sit beside me and eat breakfast," Trenton invited.

A nausea-like tidal wave rose inside her stomach and she ran from the kitchen into the bathroom.

"Mommy not feel good," she heard Trenton tell Chase.

Oh God, just what she didn't need, her son connecting with his father. If the two of them became friends, Chase would ask questions about her son's father and she didn't know how she could answer him. Sooner or later, she would get tangled up in her own lies. Right now, her body was rebelling, reminding her of all the junk she'd eaten in the last week.

Leaning over the toilet, she gagged, but never threw up. Walking back through the bedroom, she gazed longingly at the bed. Oh, to be able to lie down for another hour. There was no sick leave for moms. She had a very active little boy who needed his mother. Maybe when he napped, she could sleep then.

Headed back to the kitchen area, she noticed Chase sitting beside Trenton, both of them enjoying their cereal.

"Chase likes crunchy, too."

"Yes, I know since we're eating his cereal."

"We like crunchies," Trenton said, mimicking Chase.

Oh, dear goodness, this was not what she needed to see today. Her son imitating his father. These two should not be bonding or even liking each other. This was disaster waiting to happen.

"Trenton told me you weren't well. Are you okay?"

"Just a migraine. I'm surprised it hasn't come on before now with all the stress," she said, rubbing her forehead.

"Did you take something?"

"Some aspirin."

"From the looks of it, you need something stronger," he said. "Do you have anything?"

Well, duh, but she had a three-year-old to look after.

"I'll be fine."

"If you're worried about Trenton, I'll take care of him."

Oh no, that was a frightening thought. Not that she didn't trust him, but the idea of leaving him with his father-who didn't know he was the father—was frightening. Then again, it wasn't like Trenton could say *hey, you're my dad.*

The man was a lawyer and they had ways of digging up and finding out information. She hadn't told a soul the name of Trenton's father. And she never listed his name on the birth certificate.

With a longing glance, she looked back at the bedroom. All she had to do was take her migraine medicine, lay down for an hour or so, and usually she could kick the headache.

"Are you sure? Sometimes, he can be a handful."

"Go rest. Trenton and I are going to finish our cereal and then we'll get out his trucks."

"Watch my movie about cars."

"We'll watch his car movie," Chase said. "Go in and rest. You're pale and your eyes have a painful glow about them."

Tears welled up in her eyes but she couldn't cry. That would only make the pain worse. For him to offer to look after her son while she got rid of her headache was sweet and scary. Right now, she had no choice but to go with it because if she didn't, she would soon be throwing up and at that point, it would take her longer to recover.

"All right. I'll lie down. But not for long."

"Go right ahead. Trenton and I will be fine."

"Yes, rest, Mommy. Chase will take care of me."

For a moment, her heart cracked and she had to hurry out of the room before either one of them saw her cry.

CHASE SAT on the couch with Trenton curled up beside him, sleeping. The boy drifted off while watching his favorite movie.

The morning had been interesting, crawling all over the floor with the little guy playing trucks. Later, he'd fed him a sandwich and while normally at this time he would nap, his mother had not come out of their room. Chase was letting her sleep. She appeared exhausted.

The movie had been funny. Today felt like what it must be like with a wife and kids. Right now, his biological clock ticked at a steady pace, but someday, he wanted a family of his own. A couple of rough and rowdy boys and a sweet girl that looked like her mother, whoever she would be.

Gazing down at Trenton, he noticed the child had Laney's olive complexion and dark hair. There were other features on the child that didn't remind him of Laney and he wondered at the boy's father. Soon, hopefully in the next day or two, he would learn and could go after the man who walked away from the boy and Laney.

The door to the bedroom opened and a sleepy Laney stepped out. "I'm so sorry. How many hours did I sleep?"

"Most of the day," he said, thinking she once again had color in her cheeks.

"Oh my, I'm so sorry," she said. "Why didn't you wake me?"

"And disturb him?" he asked.

Glancing down at her son sound asleep, his head on Chase's arm, her eyes darkened, and for a moment, he thought she was going to cry.

Clearing her throat, she said, "I hope he wasn't too much trouble."

Chase laughed, remembering how he entertained the child. "No trouble at all. After this morning, I have more respect for mothers than before. He's been asleep for almost two hours. You're a very lucky woman."

And she was. Chase couldn't remember when he had so much fun crawling on the floor with trucks and a kid. After lunch, the boy insisted Chase sit beside him. So they watched a movie about talking cars and even Chase enjoyed it. Once the child grew still, his tired body relaxed and he coasted off to dreamland.

Laney carefully sank down next to Trenton and him. As she gazed at Trenton, she reached out and ran her hand along his forehead.

"Being a single mom was never part of my plan. But here I am, and my life is much richer because of this little man. Some days it's a struggle, but the joy is always there," she said staring at the child.

Mindful of his own apartment and lonely life, Chase felt jealousy flow through his veins. A vivacious little boy who loved her and kept her busy; all he had was a girlfriend who believed monogamy was outdated. The fact she still pursued him, according to Brie, was outrageous.

If anything, the last few days he focused less on the hurt and anger and more about what was missing from his life and what he wanted. In the future, this was the life he dreamed of having. A wife and family, not a relationship where he shared his woman. While monogamy might be old fashioned for others, for him, it was the only option.

"Your boy is an awesome kid," he said as a major crash happened in the movie.

"Why aren't you married with a family of your own?" she asked.

With a shrug, he stared in her big emerald eyes. "The right person hasn't come along. Sure, I date and every time I think it's about to turn serious, something happens. Obviously, I'm not choosing wisely. My dating life revolves around women with issues or weird idiosyncrasies."

A grin crossed her face and she sank further on the sofa.

"Why does that make you smile? That's not the response I'm looking for. Feel sorry for me and point out to me what's wrong with my psyche for me to choose female saboteurs."

"How would I know why you're selecting someone all wrong for you? Besides, I can't solve my own dating issues."

The image of her at the door, in a wedding dress that looked like it came out of a horror movie, made him chuckle. "Yes, I guess you do. Why didn't you know he was already married?"

"It had to have happened at his bachelor party. A group of him and his friends all went to Vegas for the weekend. Honestly, in my head, I replayed the scenario a thousand times and I don't think he did it intentionally. The break-up was for the best."

Shocked, he turned and stared at her. "What makes you say that?"

"Your sister Ally made me realize the night before the ceremony that maybe I was settling. Then again, I don't think I've ever been crazy in love."

Stunned at her revelation, he asked. "Then why did you agree to marry him?"

With a sigh, she glanced down at her son. "A year has passed since I graduated college, and I'm still living with my parents. Trenton needs a male figure in his life other than my father. Roger was nice. I thought I loved him, but looking back, I'm not certain I know what love feels like."

Looking into his eyes, she asked, "Have you ever been in love?"

That was a hard question to answer. Dating was fun, being with someone enjoyable, but the *I can't live without you* feeling had yet to come along. The *I don't want to wake up and you not be by my side.* Or his parents' steadfast devotion that no matter what came about in life, they'd always be there for each other kind of love.

"No, can't say any of my dates were someone I wanted to spend the rest of my life with. Sure, in school, I dated a lot of girls, slept with a few of them, but never found anyone I longed to put a ring on her finger. Now, I'm at the point where I want the right woman to marry and have kids with. My idea of marriage is one man, one woman, not the open concept."

A laugh rippled from her, the sound sending a tingle up his spine. When she was easy going and not ripping his head off, he liked her. Yet, she had been through a traumatic event in the last few days, she deserved a break.

Their timing was really lousy and he just happened to be the person who answered the door and she received his frustration. Not exactly his best behavior.

"Oh no. Not happening with this girl," she said. "Do you understand how many men run when I tell them about my son. Roger, he didn't mind that I had a child."

"So here we sit, on a Wednesday night, a couple of relationship rejects, watching a child's movie about automobiles and wondering why we are still single."

Her brow drew together in a frown as she smiled at him. "Maybe you're right. Maybe the God of Love put a curse on us when I danced naked around the fountain and you picked me up. Maybe we are meant for each other."

Laughing at him, he realized she was joking. "And maybe I'll win the lottery tomorrow."

"Maybe."

Trenton opened his eyes and stretched. "Mommy," he called, and wrapped his arms around her and snuggled into her chest.

Why did Chase want to be in that spot? Why did he envy a three-year-old whose mother curled around him, comforting him?

And why did he want that damn superstition to really work.

CHAPTER 6

*T*he next day, her cell phone rang for the first time in days. Glancing at the number, she saw Ally's picture and took the call.

"Hey, you," her friend said. "How are you doing?"

"Other than the fact that I've been stuck in this cabin since Saturday night, I'm fine."

"What?" Ally said, her voice rising.

Quickly, she told her about the flood waters covering the bridge and how they became trapped, carefully leaving out the part about Chase being at the lake home. Ally knew her brother picked Laney up after their Cupid dance years ago, but believed nothing ever came from their encounter.

And that was just the way Laney wanted her friend to continue thinking. Ally wasn't dumb, and every day Laney felt shocked no one had figured out Trenton's father.

"The water is receding and this afternoon we're planning on going into town."

"Oh my God, I'm so, so sorry. The river gets up occasionally, but never for days. Normally the high water lasts for a couple of hours before it drains away."

"Really, the stormy weather was a good thing--" Laney stopped, remembering Chase didn't want anyone to know he was here.

When she learned she was pregnant, she wanted Chase to tie the knot with her, but now she regarded him as a nice, attractive man. Time to put her foolish, girlish notions of marriage and forever after behind her. Suck it up and move on. Oh, who was she kidding. Even today, she was attracted to Chase, but didn't want heartache a second time.

In her short life, she never dreamed of having a baby out of wedlock and never imagined herself as a runaway bride. Both things happened to her. Life had a way of throwing obstacles in your path.

"Well, be thankful you left town. Roger's been busy stirring up trouble," Ally told her. "Your grandmother decked him with her cane when he wouldn't leave your parents' house."

"Oh no, you don't mess with my grandmother," Laney said, prickles of alarm trickling down her spine. Don't mess with the crazy woman who would stand and fight for her loved ones. A sharp mind and even sharper tongue, she would set you straight if she thought you'd done something wrong, but they all loved her passion for life.

"Now, he's harassing me," Ally admitted.

"What's he done? He's left me countless messages and apologized a lot."

The man was starting to cross a line and she would call the law on him in a heartbeat if he didn't back off.

"After he realized you were not going to answer your phone, he came to my house, certain you were hiding out here. Then he demanded that I tell him where he could find you," she said.

Roger could be overbearing, but she didn't think he would harm her friend, but still Ally shouldn't have to handle her cheating groom. Especially one she wanted to ease out of her life.

"Call the law if you need to. Don't let him intimidate you."

"Oh, I can handle him. I lied," she said flatly. "Told him I had no clue where you went or who you were with. That I wasn't your keeper."

"Thank you," she said. "Not that you should lie, but I'm so happy you didn't let him know my location. Has he been bugging you terribly?" she asked.

"A phone call every day. A visit every few days and he's practically camped out in your parents' front yard. Your mother said he comes by every afternoon trying to catch you at their house after they promised him you'd left town."

Dealing with a crazed fiancé had to be stressful for her aging parents. They didn't need the aggravation and neither did Ally. Why should her friend deal with her crazy ex-fiancé?

"Every day he calls and leaves a message. All the way from I'm sorry, to I'm going after my wife and make it work since you refuse to call me back. Frankly, I thought that eventually this would die down and he would go away. It appears he's going to force me to confront him and it's not going to be pretty."

Knowing Roger, he would tell her this was all a big misunderstanding. But her family and friends didn't deserve his harassment.

"I'll call him, but I'm not telling him where I'm at. Even with the bridge covered and us unable to leave, this time has been peaceful," she said. Since she and Chase put their differences behind them, being trapped in the cabin had been calming the last few days. He'd been so sweet to watch Trenton while she got some much needed rest and let her headache medicine work.

"What have you and the kiddo been doing?"

Oh no, what could she say? Your brother is a great entertainer? So badly, she wanted to tell her that Chase was here, but she would honor his request.

"We've been reading and watching movies and just resting," she said, which was the truth.

"Glad you're there and not here facing Roger, the Rebounder."

"Thanks, Ally, for getting me out of there. As much as I didn't want to come, I can't imagine being back home and having to face him every day. Any sight of his blonde bombshell?"

Ally chuckled. "Well, what I heard through the grapevine is that he told her to get out of town and find a lawyer."

"Hmmm...sounds like the perfect solution for him, but the message he left on my phone was that he was going to Vegas with her. Then he called back crying and said he only wanted to wound me. What he doesn't realize is, he no longer has the ability to hurt me. I'm done."

"Thank goodness he screwed up," Ally said, taking her side.

She should never have agreed to this marriage. What a colossal aberration.

"You were right and now Roger is in the past. The wedding was a mistake from start to finish. Now, he needs to stay out of my life."

And she meant it. With Roger, she settled to provide her son a father and a partner to help raise her child. All the wrong reasons for a wedding. Maybe she would never marry or maybe...stop. Like a cell door slamming shut, she refused to envision what her mind wanted her to consider. Just no.

"Later tonight, when everyone is in bed, I'll call him and tell him to leave my family and friends alone. We're over. There is no recovering from him marrying that bimbo in Vegas. No recovery."

"Everyone?"

Oh crap! Somehow, she had to fix her error. "After Trenton goes down, after my first glass of wine, but before my second, then I'm going to call Roger and we're going to talk."

LATER THAT EVENING, after Trenton was in bed, Chase

and her sat in the hot tub on the back deck, gazing out at the stars, drinking a class of wine, relaxing. Since she'd arrived, tonight was their first opportunity to soak in the tub due to the storms.

Laying her head back, she let the bubbles massage her muscles, easing the aches and pains and the tensions from her tired body. Chasing a three-year-old took a lot of energy.

"Tell me something completely inappropriate about yourself?"

With his comment, her eyes popped open and she stared at him. "What brought that up?"

A smile crossed his face. "When I watch you interacting with Trenton, you're a good mother. There's a steadiness about you."

"And boring..."

"No, not boring. But you're different. More mature."

"That's easy and you know the most inappropriate thing I've ever done. Dancing naked around the Cupid statue and staying out all night with you."

Raising his wine glass, he laughed. "What made us decide to go hiking in the moonlight?"

"It was a dare. No girl would go into the woods in the dark. Frankly, I think it was a ploy and it worked, right up until we realized we were lost and going in circles."

"That night, you lost more than one dare," he said with a laugh.

Determined there would be no discussion about what happened that night, she ignored his comment. Yes, more than one taunt had gotten her in trouble. Though Chase couldn't realize Trenton was conceived while they were lost, and she had no doubts about the father, because there had never been another man.

Staying with him that night was a challenge to stay warm without a sleeping bag or a fire. Nine months later, Trenton arrived because of their canoodling.

No one interested her enough to take the risk of creating

another child. No one, not even Roger left her trembling with passion and eager to satisfy the need.

"Thank goodness those early morning fishermen made enough noise we spotted the boat ramp and made our way out," she said. Luckily, her parents hadn't caught her coming in that morning, or they would know who was Trenton's father. But she snuck in and no one was the wiser.

"So, tell me something inappropriate about yourself?" she asked.

He chuckled. "About the worst thing I do is work fifty to sixty hours a week and occasionally go to a football game. Not one for being out of control, alcohol is not a problem. Bars are too noisy, and frankly, I'm kind of a home body."

"Remember, the night you picked me up from the Cupid statue, I asked you if you'd ever run naked and you laughed and said something about I could expect a cold day. Now I understand why. You're not really a risk taker," she said with a laugh, understanding part of his determination to get his law degree.

"You're the one who ran around the granite statue, do you believe?"

According to superstition, if they both believed, they would be each other's true loves. Because of the secrets between them, that would never happen.

"For the superstition to be real, you and I would be married and that's not going to happen. Sometimes the magic just doesn't work for everyone."

Leaning her head back against the tub, she let the warm water wash over her body, pushing the troubling thoughts away.

Sighing, she opened her eyes and glanced at him. Memories of helping each other while they tried to find their way out of the woods, until the kissing started and never stopped. Not since that night had she been kissed so thoroughly as when Chase kissed her. Even the quick kiss they shared the other day didn't compare to the desire created that night.

"Later, at times you seemed a little standoffish. We had fun together and I have nothing but pleasant memories, yet you appeared angry."

Of course, she was furious. Enraged didn't begin to describe how hurt his avoidance left her reeling. The resolution she'd arrived at that afternoon watching his taillights disappear was, he didn't want any responsibility for what occurred between them.

"I was angry at Trenton's father," she replied, which wasn't a lie. Chase didn't realize she was disappointed and hurt at how he'd been so focused on leaving for law school. After promising to call, he hadn't contacted her until she sought him out the day he left. Thus, he drove off to fulfill his dreams, knowing nothing about her pregnancy.

Lifting her wine glass to her lips, she had just taken a sip when he said, "That's understandable. You know, I'll help you get child support from his father."

Unable to stop herself, she spewed the alcohol and then pretended to be choked as his words rolled over her. Oblivious to the obvious information right in front of him, the man was stinking blind.

"No help needed," she said flatly. "We're doing just fine and I want nothing to do with Trenton's father."

Nodding, they sat there for few more moments and she drank thinking this night had been full of enlightenment. Maybe she should run before anything else was revealed.

"The bridge is no longer under water, so we'll be heading back in the morning," she announced.

"Why? Why are you going to return to let Roger harass you and try to guilt you into marrying him?"

With stunning clarity, she grasped she did feel remorse with regards to Roger, but she would never marry him. His constant harassment of Ally and her parents left her feeling guilty for being out of his reach. Once she returned, at least he wouldn't bother them, but instead her.

"He's harassing your sister and my parents. I need to put an end to his badgering. Time to face reality and realize there will never be a wedding."

"Why don't you call Roger and talk to him? See if he's willing to listen to reason. If not, I dare you to stay here with me another week. A week we could visit the town of Bride and you could thank the jilted woman for your circumstance."

Just an hour ago, she told Ally she would call Roger. Part of her wanted to remain here with Chase while the more logical side said run. The danger of him finally realizing that night they created Trenton was a very real threat.

Laney recognized she had a problem refusing a dare. Right now, he didn't have a clue Trenton was his. What if he put two and two together and came up with nine months later she had a baby?

Gritting her teeth, she didn't want to leave, she really didn't, but she should call Roger first and figure out how safe it was to return home.

"Okay, I'll agree to stay depending on how my conversation with Roger goes. Once he realizes we're done, I'm leaving. If not, then I'll take your dare and stay another week."

As she rose from the hot tub, he smiled that grin that made her toes curl every time. "I'm going to dry off and make the call."

"Good luck," he said.

And she couldn't help but think she was going to need it.

❧

AN HOUR LATER, Chase walked into the living room from the patio. He'd waited and waited for her to return, but she never did and finally went in search of her. Opening the door, he saw her sitting on the couch in the dark sniffling.

"What happened?" he asked, sitting down beside her.

"The wedding disaster, his impromptu Vegas wife, all

67

my fault," she said. "Roger blames me for everything. His marriage, us breaking up, even Miss July blonde bombshell. I'm to blame for him sleeping with her. If I had sex with him, then he wouldn't have cheated."

Chase started laughing. "Oldest man whore trick in the book. Always push the guilt off on your partner when you've been caught. Don't be fooled by this guy's words. He's the one who chose to take his dick out and put it somewhere he shouldn't."

Long ago, Chase had seen this used in divorce cases by both sides. Always shift the condemnation onto the other person. It was all in the spin and whether or not you could convince the jury to your side.

With a swipe of her hand, she wiped her eyes. "Yes, I know, but still I feel bad. All the money we spent on that ceremony only to have it end the way it did."

"It's cheaper than a divorce," he said, thinking of his clients he represented during their divorces. Eventually he went into criminal law to escape the ugliness of broken relationships. At least with a criminal, you had a chance of proving them innocent, but the breakup of a marriage was ugly.

Tears streamed down her face, his chest tightening at the anguish reflected from her emerald gaze. "He said he was going to make me pay for his part of the event unless we got back together. When I responded and told him that was not happening, that we would never be married, he told me to..."

A sob escaped her throat. "Once again, I screwed up my life."

Pulling her into his arms, he locked her against him, comforting her, wanting to ease her pain, wanting her to realize the man didn't deserve her. Breathing in her sweet essence, he started to press soft kisses against her neck as he rubbed her back. "Shhh, you're just having a rough time."

"This is so unfair," she said. "This is the second time I've made the wrong decision."

Holding her, he let her cry. As her sobs finally ended, he leaned back and looked in her teary eyes. "You all right?"

Nodding, unable to say anything, her dark green eyes widened, her pupils dilated as she licked her lips. Desire ripped from his chest sending his scorching blood racing through his veins.

"Oh hell," he said as his mouth covered hers.

It was a kiss he'd held back for days. Waiting and wondering if there were any real feelings, or if they were responding on the rebound. This passion punch of their mouths, had nothing to do with rebound. This kiss was filled with anticipation and wonder and enough tingles that below his waist had perked up, signaling approval.

She tasted of wine and dreams and something that triggered a long ago memory. A flash of the two of them entwined, lying on his jacket, the hoot of an owl overhead and a thousand stars their canopy. The smell of the forest, the caress of the cool breeze swept over him as she pushed him back, her breath raspy and harsh sounding in the darkened room.

For a moment, they sat staring at each other in bewilderment. This was a bone melting lips smacker that made the one outside the other day look like child's play. This melding of the lips was one step away from the bedroom.

"We can't do this," she gasped.

Chase didn't respond, knowing she was right, but not caring. Both of them existed in a tenacious place right now, but still the hunger, the connection growing between them seemed right. The feel of Laney in his arms seemed natural, and although he wasn't a man who normally recognized his emotions, that kiss felt like a homecoming, a place he belonged.

With his arms around her, her breasts crushed against his chest the need to take her right there on the couch filled him. But he realized that would send her fleeing.

"Tell me why you think you screwed up again?"

CHAPTER 7

*L*eaning back, she stared at him, her arms wrapped around his chest. Her lips tingled with a deliciousness that brought memories back from their night in the woods. The place where she gave him a small piece of her heart only for him to trample on it.

"Isn't it obvious?" she said with an incredulous look on her face.

"Who is the father?"

Pushing the rest of the way back, she leaned away. All the desire burning inside her shriveling in to a cold ball within her chest. Right now, it would be so easy to tell him the truth, but she feared for her son.

Rising from the couch, she put distance between them, needing space to keep from letting all her pent-up frustration explode on him.

"If I won't tell my own mother and father, what makes you think I'm going to tell you? It's irrelevant. He's out of the picture. The baby is just the result of a one-night stand gone bad."

All the lies to maintain her son's safety. For her, college was not about partying or dating or even learning about relationships, but taking her classes and getting home to Trenton. There were no one-night stands in her past and the only man she ever slept with seemed clueless.

What was she doing? First Chase, then Jim, next Roger, and now back to Chase? Maybe she should walk away from men since she had bad luck with them.

"Okay, I understand. That doesn't explain to me why you think you screwed up your life again. So, you got pregnant in college, happens to girls all the time. Don't blame yourself for this wedding fiasco; it could be for the best."

Of course, she did. Only once again, she had been trying to make it up to her son because he didn't have a father. At first, she believed Roger would be the perfect man to father her boy and how did that turn out?

"Yes, I do. Maybe I should have had sex with him." But she knew that was a lie.

"Do you want Roger? Are you certain you are willing to put up with him in sickness and health?"

"No," she said quietly, knowing how lucky she learned his nature before the vows were said. The man cheated on her before they married, what would he do after?

"Are you ready to return home and deal with him again?"

No, she didn't want to leave, but being here was so dangerous. Not only to her son, but also her heart. When they created Trenton, she wasn't in love with Chase, but infatuated and that ended badly. Seven more days here alone with him, how would her heart fare then?

"No."

"Frankly, I see a woman who not only had a child, she's raising him by herself, and she finished her degree. If I was your man, I would be damn proud of who you are and what you've done."

His words were like a balm to her soul, making her realize with her family's help and her determination, she had accomplished a lot. And would do more, very soon. Now, she needed to hibernate from the drama of going home.

Staring at him, she wondered, if he learned the truth, how would he really feel? The tension had drained her, leaving her frustrated and she refused to say much more.

That kiss left her reeling and she longed for time to process what was happening between them. Could she be responding on the rebound or the man she secretly considered her own was fulfilling her dreams, only to break her heart again?

"If you're running because I kissed you, let me remind you, I dared you to stay and you said yes."

How long before she learned not to be so dumb? Taunts did nothing but get her into trouble, yet she couldn't refuse one.

"Damn you for daring me. That always gets to me."

"Always has, even when we were kids. Not my problem," he said, grinning at her.

What could she do? She wanted to stay here, but because of Trenton, she would need to be cautious. No matter what, her boy remained her top priority. Anything she did could bring no harm to her son.

The rest of the world, including Roger, would have to wait. Laney needed a break to recover, recoup, and grow stronger.

❧

THOUGH IT WAS LATE, he knew his secretary would not be upset if he called her. Still it was after ten.

"Chase, there had better be blood somewhere to be calling me this late," Brie said answering the phone. "What if I was married and had a man here? What if you had interrupted us?"

Grinning into the phone, he knew she wasn't really upset with him, yet he did take advantage of her.

"Oh, Brie, I knew you were up watching television. And if you'd had a man there, you wouldn't have answered the phone."

A beautiful woman, Brie had just as much trouble with dates as Chase. When they began to work together, they agreed it would only be a working relationship, nothing more. And so far, they sympathized with one another, but they had not crossed that line.

"Dang, you're right. But it's a good thing you pay me well or I wouldn't be putting up with this crap."

"I know. But it's also why you're so good at your job. You are my right hand and take good care of me."

She sighed in the phone and he knew he'd won her over.

"What is it you need?" she asked.

"What have you learned about the birth certificate?"

"You are not going to like what I tell you," she said. "There is no name listed. That child doesn't have a father according to the state."

A curse escaped from his lips. "How am I supposed to find this asshole and make him pay if she didn't list him on the certificate? That doesn't make sense."

"Maybe the woman doesn't want anyone to know who the daddy is," she said. "Maybe it's for the best that no one knows for the child's safety."

What if that was true? What if his interfering did more harm than good? What if Trenton's father was a mobster or what if Laney had been raped and the child was a product of that assault? When they spoke about the father, she acted like she never wanted to see him again, but was that her pride talking or was it true?

"I'm going to the store to get a DNA test kit. Talk to my friend, Dr. Goodman, at the medical examiner's office and ask him to run the DNA. Just as soon as I can, I'll get you the kit."

There was a moment of silence on the phone. "Boss, think about what you're doing. You're going behind this woman's back trying to find the father of her child. Have you asked her permission?"

"No, I think she will be relieved when I locate him and make the bastard start paying child support."

Silence filled the airways and he knew she was thinking of ways to present her case in a logical manner. This is what they did for one another. Always challenging and presenting both sides of the cases they worked on together.

"Sometimes women don't want their baby daddy to know about the child. You could be making a huge mistake."

The different scenarios ran through his mind of why she would want to keep the child a secret from the father. "We don't know what we're going to find. Let's just see if we turn up anything. Before I contact the father, I'll tell her. That way she can decide if she wants him to know."

"I still don't like you doing this. I think it's wrong, but at least, before you contact the father, you're talking to her. What if she's in the witness protection program or something because this man threatened her?"

He started laughing. "You need to write suspense novels. At night, your mind comes up with some strange scenarios. This girl went to school with me and was my sister's best friend. She's not in the witness protection program."

"If I wrote novels, then you wouldn't have me as your secretary. And believe me, no one else would put up with your crazy girlfriend."

Oh, he had hoped that Cissy would have given up on getting him back by now. Maybe he should introduce her to Roger. They could make each other miserable.

"She's still calling the office?"

"Every day she calls and wants to know when you'll be back."

Anger clenched his stomach. Did the woman ever give up?

"You have my permission to tell her that Chase said as far as she was concerned, he would never be back in town for her," he said, then stopped. "That's not fair. I shouldn't drag you into my personal business."

She chuckled. "Oh, boss, it would be a pleasure to tell this woman to ride off into the sunset and never return. Believe me, I can do this."

"You don't have to. I'm going to contact her right now and tell her to lose my number."

"Good luck with that. She's one determined woman."

Why did it seem that when he stepped away and wanted nothing else to do with Cissy, she suddenly couldn't live without him and yet she had been the one all cozied up with the MMA fighter?

He touched his sore ribs. No, there was no way he was going back there.

The image of Laney came to mind and the memory of their shared kiss tonight. When their lips touched, he had only one thought. He wanted Laney Baxter. He wanted her in his bed - rebound or not, she would soon be his.

THE NEXT MORNING, Laney was nervous as they prepared to cross the rain swollen river. Before they crawled in the truck, she insisted Chase put the life jackets in the back seat, where Trenton sat in his car seat.

They were going to town in Chase's truck, not her car because of the height off the ground. As they neared the bridge, she noticed the mud and debris left behind by the rushing water.

"Are you certain it's safe?"

"It looks sturdy," he said. "We'll be fine."

He drove slowly over the concrete road and she couldn't help but feel relieved when they reached the other side.

"Safe and sound," he said looking at her and grinning. "We didn't need the life jackets."

"Thank goodness, but it never hurts to be prepared."

A smile crossed his face and he patted her on the knee,

sending a delicious shiver through her. That old spark of tempting attraction had reawakened and now she wondered if she should have stayed. But she also wasn't ready to go home and face the situation there.

"Once again, you're showing your girl scout training," he said, teasing her.

"And you were always the little boy stopping the bullies. Seems like you're still standing up for justice."

With a quick shrug, he gazed at her. "What can I say? I can't stand to see people taken advantage of. Fairness is one of the reasons I became a lawyer."

Somehow she was going to spend the next week with him, not letting this chemistry grow any stronger. That was going to be a tall order to fill. Because just looking at him sitting beside her driving, she wanted to tug his lips down to hers and run her tongue over their fullness.

"So where are we going this morning?" she asked. "Trenton will wear out on us by one or two o'clock and need a nap," she said.

"No nap. I'm a big boy," he told her from the back seat.

"Yes, you're my little man," she told him. "You don't have to go to sleep. We'll watch one of your movies."

Chase glanced at her from behind the wheel of the truck. "So sly. He'll fall asleep watching his show," he said softly.

"Most of the time," she said. "A movie is easier than fighting him to go to sleep. Turn on his car show and off he goes."

A grin crossed his face. "Well, I thought we'd start off at Two Cups. Let's get a cup of coffee and a muffin or pastry and make a list of food. Then if you want, we could walk through the small downtown area visiting the antique shops and specialty stores. Afterward, we'll finish off the day at the grocery store."

Chase parked his truck in front of the café. Laney hopped out and looked up and down the street of the quaint town. Bride, Texas, reminded her of the small towns on television in favorite sitcoms. As soon as Trenton was released, the child scampered out.

As he hopped down, she went to grab his hand and missed, but Chase scooped up the little boy before he had the chance to run onto the road. Her lungs seized causing her to gasp. "Trenton, you must wait and take my hand..."

"Muffin, Mommy," he called.

Chase carried him in his arms, her heart pounded in her chest as she swallowed hard, trying to ease the lump in her throat. Father and son went together. They looked so natural, and for the first time, she realized Trenton had a lot of the same features as his dad.

Opening the door, they stepped inside out of the hot sun and into the cool bakery. Trenton spotted the case of muffins and screeched with delight.

"Muffin, Mommy," he said again as she tried to compose herself. What was she doing here in Bride, Texas, with his father? Why had she accepted that crazy dare? Would she never learn?

"What kind do you want?" she asked.

"Down, Chase, down," the little boy demanded.

Chase set him down, smiled at Laney. "Don't get between the boy and his muffins."

The child placed his tiny hands on the glass case and leaned in close to determine his choice. This little man was such a character that she would protect with her life.

"That one, Momma, that one," he said, pointing to a gooey cinnamon with sugar icing. Just the stuff to hype him up. The kid had been so good being confined in the house. "On one condition. At lunch, you have to eat some veggies."

"Me will," he said, his eyes glued on the girl behind the counter who pulled out his muffin.

"You guys must be visiting from out of town," the woman said. "Don't remember seeing you here before."

"My family owns Casa Leon River cabin," Chase said. "The river's been out of its banks and today is the first day we've been able to cross the bridge."

"That last storm was a doozy," the lady said. "What else for you folks?"

"Two cups of coffee and a couple of those cookies," Chase said, gazing at a gooey snickerdoodle in the counter.

"No, I didn't want anything but coffee," Laney said, gazing at him.

"Wait, you'll be thanking me after you taste these cookies," he said.

Laney tried to pay for their breakfast but Chase pushed her hand away. "My treat."

"No arguments. I'm getting groceries," she said.

There was no response, but she knew that was his way of not provoking her, but that didn't necessarily mean yes.

"I'll bring these out to you," she said.

Taking a seat at the table, Laney put Trenton in a booster chair sitting next to her. Glancing around at the bustling coffee shop, she could tell many of the patrons lived in the town.

"Just a moment, I'll be right back," Chase said and walked toward the men's room.

Just then the woman brought their order to them. She gazed at Laney.

"So, you going to be staying long in Bride?"

"Oh no," Laney told her.

"Your husband's family owns a cabin on the river. Those are so hard to come by these days," she said.

"Hmmm, Chase is not my husband. He's a friend," she said, feeling flustered. The waitress seemed overly interested in them, but maybe they were this friendly with everyone. In case Roger was searching, Laney didn't want to draw a lot of attention to herself.

The girl sat down across from her. "Be sure to go by and see the Bride statue and read the story of Ellora Shepherd," she said. "Our little town is a haven for jilted brides and second chances at love. If you're looking for love, we have a very good matchmaker. Visit Nancy Redd down on 44th Street. Let her fix you up."

Stunned, Laney stared. Why in the world would she tell her about a matchmaker? Did she look desperate? She started to tell her the truth, but decided no use in letting everyone know of her humiliation. For all she knew, this woman spread gossip like she spread icing on the muffins.

"Here in Bride, the women stick together and try to let others know about our town's past," she said as if reading her mind.

"By the way, I'm Carol Lane, I own this here joint."

Laney stared at the woman about her age. "Nice to meet you. Why should I go see this matchmaker?"

"Oh, honey, Nancy Reed has a matchmaking record a mile long. Half the people in this town have been hitched because of that woman." With a smile, she said, "Can't hurt to try. That is if you want to be married."

What a dilemma. Of course, Laney wanted to marry and for Trenton to have a father, but she had gone through a disastrous split. A lightbulb went off in her head.

"Tell me, do you know if she can tell if you're already in love with someone? How could she match you with the right person if your heart belonged to someone else?"

The woman smiled and stood. "Go see her. Ask her that question. She may have the answer you're looking for."

Walking away, all Laney could think about was the man who approached the table. With every day they were together, she pondered more and more if they were meant for each other after all.

CHAPTER 8

*C*limbing back in the truck, he glanced around at the main street. "Next stop the grocery store?"

Laney turned to him. "While you were in the bathroom, the waitress told me about the tribute to Ellora Shepherd. Could we go by the statue? I'd like to learn how this little town became known as Bride, Texas."

Chase didn't mind going to see the town's rock sculpture of the strong woman. When he was a kid, every cousin or friend that came to the house had to visit the memorial when they came to town. It had been years since he'd seen the carved granite of the woman who created Bride.

"Let's go," he said as he whipped the vehicle out onto the two-lane road.

The boy giggled from his car seat in the back, "Cars, Chase."

"Yes, just like in your movie," he said.

"Go fast," the child taunted.

"Can't, buddy. We're in town and there might be a little boy or girl crossing the street. We must go slow," he said as he pulled into a parking space near the town square.

"That was quick. Why didn't we walk?"

"You're right, but I thought we were going to the store," he said.

"Do you mind?" she asked.

Of course, he didn't mind. Spending time with her and Trenton, he enjoyed being together, but he wanted to sneak off to the pharmacy and pick up the DNA kit.

"No. Come on, let's go see the statue and read her story," he said.

Lifting Trenton out of the car seat, they each took a hand and he walked between them, swinging their hands and giggling as he gazed at the adults.

"Momma, is Chase my daddy?"

Glancing at her, Chase noticed the stricken expression on her face and couldn't stop the smile from spreading as he observed her complexion turn pale. Trying to compose herself, she swallowed, her emerald eyes growing wide.

"Honey, no, Chase is just a friend."

The child gazed up at his mother confused. "But you like him, Momma," he asked.

"Yes, I like him," she said and Chase grinned at her.

Laney was having a hard time admitting she liked him. Even with her own son. The tension on her face almost made him laugh; he enjoyed seeing her squirm.

"Good, I like him, too," he said grinning at Chase.

A warmth spread through his chest as he stared down at the child he wanted to help. No, Brie would not talk him out of helping this young man. The boy deserved to know who his father was.

Reaching the memorial, he watched as Laney read the history of Ellora Shepherd and how she overcame diversity to build the town.

"That's so sad. The plaque says she eventually married another man and had children. Another jilted bride."

"That one has a happy ending," he reminded her. "Maybe you

will, too."

An uneasy feeling gripped his stomach at the image of a man marrying her.

Suddenly Trenton yanked on her arm.

"Momma, bikes. Ride bikes," Trenton said, jumping up and down.

Chase looked over to where the boy was pointing to the park. A bike rental place where you could rent a bicycle and peddle around the trails at the edge of the square. The last time he'd ridden had been in college. The idea of the three of them tootling along through the trees sounded like fun.

A quick glance at Laney and it was odd the way they communicated in silence, without speaking. Even before she said a word, Chase concluded she wanted to go bicycling. But he asked just the same.

"Do you want to go bike riding?" he asked.

"Only if they have a booster seat and a helmet for Trenton."

The little boy jumped up and down excitedly as they crossed the street to the vendor.

In a matter of moments, they were all on bicycles, wearing helmets and ready to go for a ride. Chase insisted Trenton sit behind him. At first, she argued, but when he used the reasoning that the child was heavy and he had more strength than she did to make certain they balanced. At last, she agreed.

For the next hour, they rode through the trees, enjoying being outside, laughing and acting like a family. A family that Chase dreamed of having someday. Finally, they stopped to rest, and he was surprised they had ridden so long. A yawning Trenton made him realize the boy was starting to tire.

"Guess, we better take these back to the rental place since our time is up in ten minutes," he said.

"This has been fun. I'm glad we did this," she said.

At that moment, the memory of the two of them sitting on a rock in the woods, in the darkness, wondering if they should hunker down for the night or continue searching for their way back to the car.

Gazing at her, he remembered how her skin sparkled in the moonlight, but staring at her now, he thought her even more beautiful and had the most incredible urge to kiss her.

A tired little boy followed their every move and they needed to return to the booth.

They took off again and this time they rode a little faster.

"Look, Momma, look. Chase is making us fly," the boy called to his mother who was directly behind them.

"You're speeding," she yelled.

Turning his head, he glanced behind at her and quickly realized his mistake. The bike wobbled and he tried to bring it back under control, but when he hit a ridge of jagged rock, the front wheel came off the sidewalk and they plummeted to the ground. Though the path was concrete, he pushed the vehicle away from himself hoping Trenton would land on the soft grass.

"Trenton!" he heard Laney screaming and then he bounced hard on the terrain. His lungs screamed in pain as he landed on the ground, the breath knocked out of him. Trenton.

Kneeling, he shook the cobwebs from his brain and searched for the child.

Laying on the grass, he didn't move. Chase feared he killed him. Like a snail, he crawled to the boy's side where Laney knelt beside him, checking on the child.

"I knew I should have had him ride with me. Why did I trust my son with you? Look at him, he's not moving," she cried.

Chase's chest tightened with fear, his ribs thundering with pain, his whole body aching. No no no... Chase cared about this kid and his injuries would be his fault. Trenton couldn't be dead or seriously hurt or anything. He just couldn't.

The boy started coughing and they stared at each other.

"Don't move, baby," Laney said softly.

A man came running over to them and kneeled down beside them on the grass. "Is everyone okay?"

Just then, Trenton slowly opened his eyes and laughed. "Want to fly again, Chase."

Laney turned and gave Chase a murderous glimpse that if she had a gun, he feared bullets would have been flying.

"I'm not sure," Laney said glancing at the man who wore a cowboy hat the color of graphite. His beard was salted with gray and his dark eyes assessed the situation.

"Do you folks need some help," he asked. "Looks like you're both pretty banged up."

A yellow lab sat off to the side, its tail wagging, impatient to continue their walk.

Part of Chase wanted to accept the man's help, but he just couldn't ask for it.

"Thanks, but I think we'll be okay," he told the man.

"My name is Gavin Redd, I live here in Bride. I'd be happy to help you," he said.

"Maybe help me stand," Chase finally admitted.

"I'm sorry, we wrecked, buddy," he said, gazing at Trenton, thinking his ribs felt like a bad conga drum corps played them and he wondered about the damage. In fact, his body ached like a Mack truck had slammed into him.

"Do you think we should take him to the ER?"

"Son, move your arms and legs for mommy," she demanded.

"Can we ride some more?" he asked, opening his eyes. "Me not hurt, don't take me home."

The tension on Laney's face was close to erupting. Chase understood she worried about her boy, he was, too, but frankly, he thought the kid had the wind knocked out of him, but was okay. If anything, the boy seemed stunned, but was quickly recovering.

"First, we need to determine if you're injured," she said leaning over him. "Move your arms and legs."

The boy moved his limbs and she said, "Open your eyes."

Though his eyes didn't appear to be dilated, he hit his head hard. There was no point in taking a chance.

"We're both going to the emergency room," Chase said, thinking his ribs burned like a branding iron rested on them. Also, it would be best if they verified the child didn't have a concussion.

"Good idea," Gavin said.

With a glance, he knew they were in agreement.

"Gavin, can you help me?"

"Sure," the lanky cowboy said and walked over as Chase slowly pulled himself up from the ground, careful not to use his arms or put any pressure on the muscles around his chest.

Rising, she watched him and he fathomed she was waiting for him to pick up Trenton, but he wasn't certain he had the strength to lift the child. Finally, he said "You grab the bikes and I'll carry Trenton."

A frown drew her forehead together. "Are you all right? You landed roughly."

"Let me carry the boy," Gavin said.

With a shallow breath, he nodded his head. "I'll be fine."

"How are your ribs? Did you land on them?"

"Smacked them pretty hard."

"Are you injured?"

"Don't know," he said as he watched Gavin lift Trenton into his arms.

Though he wanted to carry the boy, he knew his muscles would scream at him in protest. Unable to stop the sound, he gasped, but winked at Trenton, determined to get them all back to his vehicle.

"Chase, let me help you."

"No, I'm fine." That was not exactly the truth.

When they reached his truck, he handed her his keys. "You have to drive us to the ER."

"Nice to meet you, Gavin. We couldn't have made it without your help.

"I'll get these bikes back to the vendor. Hope you folks are okay. I'll see you around," the cowboy said as he ambled away.

❧

LANEY DROVE CHASE'S big truck to the small-town emergency clinic. The trick was getting Chase out of the vehicle. The man was stiff and having a hard time moving. Trenton appeared all right, but still she wanted him checked for a concussion.

They hobbled in and thankfully only one person waited ahead of them.

The clerk behind the desk looked at them and Laney knew she assumed they were together. Up until the crash, she had been imagining the three of them as a family out for an afternoon ride. One that didn't end in a crash.

"Are you the child's father?" she asked Chase.

Fear spiked rushing through her, paralyzing her lungs. "No," she said with a gasp. "Unknown."

A glance of confusion had Chase drawing his brows together, a frown gathering on his face. Shaking his head like he couldn't hear what was said.

"I'm not unknown," Chase said with a grimace. "We're not related to one another."

All she needed was for him to start questioning her about Trenton's father. Sooner or later, she feared he would stop and do the math and realize that one night, even though they used protection, they made a baby.

"Oh," the woman behind the counter said. "Sorry, I thought you guys came in together."

"We did," he said. "But we'd like different rooms."

The girl shook her head and then led them to the back. Chase went into the room next to them and Trenton grew agitated.

86

"Chase?" Trenton called starting to cry. "Want Chase."

"He'll be back," Laney said running her hand along her son's head, worried he suffered from a head injury. Knowing he was tired, but fearful of letting him fall asleep.

The door opened and the doctor stepped in and Trenton eyed him warily. "No shot."

The man nodded and held up his hands to show him there were no needles. "I agree, son, no shot."

"What happened," he asked. "Where did he hit his head?"

For the next few minutes, she went over the accident wishing the last ten minutes of the ride hadn't ruined their perfect day.

Afterward, the medical professional carefully examined her baby. "Is the father in the next room?"

Frustrated, these people seemed nosy, she had to hold in the response she wanted to give.

"No, he's not the father," she lied. "He's a friend."

"Well, tell your friend that by making this child wear a helmet, he's going to be just fine. There may be some bruising where he landed, but his eyes are clear. He follows the light and I think he's a strong little man. If he starts acting strange or has any other complications, bring him back here immediately. Good job on the helmet."

Why did the man assume Chase made him wear the protective head gear?

"Actually, I made him strap on the protection," she said, not wanting the doctor to think she was an irresponsible parent.

"Trenton, you just survived your first bike accident. There will be more. You might want to check his pupils in about an hour and make certain they're still not dilated," he said and hurried out the door.

Relief overwhelmed her and she felt tears sting her lids. Thank goodness she'd insisted he wear a helmet. That little bit of protection saved him from a much bigger injury.

Several minutes later, Chase came out of the room, moving stiffly, a couple of prescriptions in his hand.

"Is Trenton all right?" he asked, an anxious expression on his face, his eyes scanning the child.

"Unlike his mother, he's a lucky little boy," she said, trying to make light of the situation, especially after her comments were critical of Chase. "The doctor said his helmet kept him from getting injured."

"Me okay," Trenton said, his head against her shoulder. The boy was exhausted and so ready for his nap.

"What did you find out?" she asked, perceiving the bottles of pills meant something was wrong.

"The doctor thinks I reinjured my ribs and scolded me for riding bikes."

Walking closer to her, he put his hand on the small of her back, encircling the two of them. At his touch, a rush of security filled her. Like they were a unit and he comforted her instead of her reassuring him. All day, this sense of unity, of oneness, had suffused her. Now more than ever.

"Today, I had so much fun until we fell. And I'm so relieved Trenton is okay," he said and laid his head on her shoulder.

Tears welled up in her eyes as she gazed at her two men.

"Come on, I think it's time I took the wounded home," she said.

"Sleepy," Trenton said. "Time to watch movie."

Both of them laughed at him and together they begin to walk toward the door.

Trenton would be asleep before they arrived at the cabin. Chase needed to sit down. The most incredible urge to take care of him like she did Trenton came over her. Not that she wanted to treat him like a child, but she longed to make him feel better.

"Come on, guys, maybe we're safer at the cabin."

THE NEXT DAY, Laney left the two of them cuddled on the couch in front of the television watching another of Trenton's movies while she drove into town for groceries. Funny how in a week they had grown close. Too close. Because when they returned to Cupid, she didn't want Chase remembering her boy.

The last week of her life had been rather trying. First, the disastrous attempted wedding, then the flooding and being forced to stay in the cabin together, and now this bonding between father and son that frightened her. Plus, her own growing feelings toward Chase.

Though they only shared one special night, she remembered listening to him telling her about his dreams of becoming a lawyer. Chase knew his path and didn't want anyone to get in the way - not a wife and certainly not a child.

As a young woman, the memory of standing in his driveway, his family surrounding him, watching them sending him off to complete his journey caused her chest to ache.

At that moment, she realized she would not tell him about Trenton. At that very second, she made the decision to keep her son's father a secret. No one would know, but her.

While it hurt tremendously, she still stood by her decision.

Driving into Bride, she saw the restaurant where they'd stopped yesterday and remembered how the waitress had told her about Nancy Redd, matchmaker.

Why not? Roger was out of the picture and she wanted a father for her child. What if she talked to the woman? It wasn't often she had time without Trenton at her side. What if she stopped at Nancy's first and let her try to find her someone.

Pulling her car up in front of a house that could use a coat of paint, she parked out front and then ascended the steps, feeling a little nervous. After all, Roger was her second attempt at marriage and both times she struck out. Why would she want to take a chance on finding another man?

Ringing the bell, she waited at the door, her heart pounding. This was just for fun, she didn't believe in matchmakers. They were kind of like soothsayers, she didn't trust them, either.

The door opened and a woman who looked like she had to be at least eighty with gray hair and a wrinkled face stood staring at her. "Well, hi, there. You must be Laney Baxter. Come on in."

Startled that the woman knew her name, she walked into the house. "How did you know who I was? I've barely been to town."

Nancy laughed and dropped her wrist in a downward wave. "Oh honey, when someone new arrives, I have ears and eyes on the ground that tell me everything." Stopping in her living room, she turned to Laney. "Have a seat and tell me what brings you to visit?"

Laney took a deep breath, not really certain she should be consulting someone about finding her another man. But the woman had the same last name as the man who helped them yesterday. She wondered if they were related. "Do you know a Gavin Redd?"

"Yes, that's my grandson," she said.

"He helped us yesterday when we had a bike accident in the park."

"You're that young couple, he told me about."

"Yes. And the waitress at Two Cups told me you're good at matchmaking."

The woman grinned and sat in a chair across from her. "Yes, ma'am. I can pick out two people made for each other in seconds. All it takes is me learning a little something about them. I advise the woman who I think goes with that personality and soon there are wedding bells. Fifty couples are together because of my matchmaking. People in town believe in my services."

A tingle went through Laney and she frowned. What was she doing here?

"Wait a minute. Aren't you here with that good-looking

lawyer feller whose family owns the place down on the river? If so, why are you here?"

The question was relevant, but even Laney didn't understand why she wanted to talk to a matchmaker. For some reason, she believed she would give her direction with regards to men. A weak area for Laney.

"We aren't together, romantically," Laney said, knowing if she let down her walls that Chase would be back in her life.

The woman reached across the small distance and grabbed her hands. "Now, honey, I was in the park yesterday. Who did I behold riding bikes? The two of you and thought, what a nice family. Their baby is so cute."

Laney tried not to react, but Nancy tilted her gray-haired head and stared at her. "He doesn't know."

For a moment, Laney's chest squeezed and she had to resist the urge to jump up and run screaming out the door. This woman must have X-ray vision or something. "What are you talking about?"

Leaning back in her chair, she didn't release Laney's hands. "You haven't told him the boy is his."

How could a stranger perceive this? She was just spouting a conjecture.

"What does this have to do with finding me a husband?"

"Not a thing," she said, releasing her hands. "But I don't think you need me. Sure, I could tell you the names of a couple of men who would give their left nut to go out with you. Sweetie, you're not available. Personally, from what I witnessed, your heart has already been claimed."

"No," she said, shaking her head. "Just no. Once we..."

She stopped. She couldn't tell this woman, an outsider, about the night she and Chase spent together. That one night almost four years ago. The night she trusted would promise them forever, but had only gifted them with a son.

Bending forward, she patted Laney on the arm. "Something

happened between the two of you that broke you apart." She held up her hand. "Of course, I have no idea what, but one of you needs to take down your walls and give this romance a second chance. From what I see, it's you. You're afraid."

Pain gripped her chest, a sharp pain. For a moment, she thought she was having a heart attack. The realization it was fear, and the matchmaker clearly understood what drove Laney, but not that there was a small pint of a boy she had to consider.

How could Laney let down her guard and give the man another opportunity to wound her? Being vulnerable to him a second time could break her. What about Trenton?

With a clarity she seldom experienced, a voice inside her head called her out. *Liar. You've been waiting for years for him to come to his senses.*

And she had. How would he feel when he learned she hid his son from him?

"Look, honey, this is a lot to take in, but I think the two of you belong together. Even if it doesn't last, right now, you must see this through. Make certain you aren't meant for one another. First, you need to stop thinking of him as that evil man who left me alone and pregnant."

Sitting there stunned, Laney stared. In her mind, that's exactly how she thought of Chase. The malicious man who abandoned her to deal with an unplanned pregnancy, questioning parents, and loss of self-esteem.

"He's not a bad guy," the woman said and Laney wanted to ask how she knew, but didn't. This felt like she was talking to someone who had known them for years. She pegged both of them.

Staring at the woman, uneasiness flowed like a flood. Today, she came here on a whim and instead Nancy was prying open her eyes, forcing her to understand the truth. The truth she had avoided for so many years.

She stood, signaling an end to their chat. "Come back to visit me in six months and I'll find someone for you if you and the lawyer don't work out. For now, I think the man for you is right in front of you."

Regardless, of whether or not she was right, Laney needed to get out of this house. To step away to think about what she said.

"I'm not sure you're right. But if you are..."

"When you visit, we'll have some sweet tea and apple pie to celebrate your new husband."

For so long, she considered Chase as the bad guy, the idea of forgiving seemed strange. Hiding secrets from him, she would be willing to give this a try.

"Or for you to find me a man."

"Deal!" the older woman said and gave her a hug.

CHAPTER 9

wo days after the biking accident, Chase's ribs were
still sore. His legs black and blue where the bike fell
over on top of him, but he didn't care. Seeing Trenton falling
with the bicycle had taken years off his life.

The thought of him being the reason the child could have
gotten hurt made his chest ache. Funny how protective he'd
become of the tyke, even sitting through his movies while the kid
fell asleep beside him.

Now, more than ever, he was determined to learn of Trenton's father and bring him to justice. Yesterday, while Laney went
grocery shopping, he lay on the couch with Trenton watching the
crane operator movie and ordering a DNA test online.

Yes, it had been a shock you could buy the paternity kit on the
Internet. The package shipped overnight, and at any moment, the
brown truck would arrive to deliver his kit.

Hopefully, he would be able to do the swabs and send it to his
office where his secretary would handle the rest. If he called in a
few favors, the results would be in his hands in less than a
week. And then he would guide her through the legal process of

taking the bastard to court and getting the child support she needed.

Nothing could be worse than a man who didn't pay for his children. Over the years, Chase had been very careful not to get a girl pregnant. No protection, no sex.

"Chase," Trenton came running in from the bathroom. "Want to play trucks?"

"Buddy, I'd love to, but I've got the ice pack on my ribs. What if you drive them right here in front of me and I'll watch."

"Okay," he said. "But you make car go fast."

"Varoom, varoom," Chase said and the little boy giggled.

Just then, he heard the delivery truck rolling up the drive. The kit was here and soon he would know his answers. Trying to rise before the man reached the doorbell, he watched Laney come into the room.

"There's a truck outside."

"Yes, I ordered a book off Amazon. I needed something new to read."

"Oh, why didn't you say something? You're welcome to borrow one of the books I brought. You didn't have to order one."

From the couch, he gazed at her, hoping she wouldn't expect him to open it in front of her.

Meeting the man on the porch, she carried in the box. "Here you go. I'm going to finish doing laundry. Do you have anything to go in the washer?"

It felt so domesticated, so homey and right that this atmosphere left him nervous. This was what he wanted, and yet if he dated Laney, she came with a family. Not only would he be a husband, but a father. Was he ready for that kind of responsibility?

Sure, he was, but was the beautiful woman standing before him the person he was meant to spend the rest of his life with?

They enjoyed each other's company. She was fun and it

seemed easy with Laney. But the question remained, were they intended for one another?

"Earth to Chase. Clothes? Wash?"

"No, I'm good," he said. "Why don't you forget the laundry and sit here with me and Trenton and play trucks?" The need to be with her just seem to fall from his lips. Today she wore her dark mahogany hair pulled back away from her face in a ponytail, reminding him of how she looked that fateful night so long ago.

"Why, of course, I would love to crawl on the floor with the two of you," she said. "Thank you so much for the offer."

He grinned. "Trenton and I didn't want to leave you out."

No, he wanted her there at his side, close.

"Play, Mommy, play trucks."

She gave a half smile, half snort. "Let me turn on the washer and I'll be right back and we can play."

There was something about the way she had a glow about her that attracted him. Yesterday she came back a solemn expression on her face and he wasn't certain if the cause was leaving Trenton with him for the first time or if something else troubled her.

As she walked out of the room, the most incredible urge to rip open the box, pull out the swabs and test the boy overcame him. Why did he ask her to play trucks with them? Why hadn't he waited until she was in the utility room and done the swab?

Because he really wanted her by his side. The smell of her drifting over him as they sat side by side on the couch had him wanting to experience that kiss again. In fact, he wanted to be alone with her, but knew he had to wait until tonight. Then he intended to kiss her and show her his feelings.

Glancing up, she strolled back in the room. "Let's get truck-ing," she said and dropped onto the floor beside her son who glanced up at her adoring the fact they were all going to drive trucks.

Let the fun begin.

PLAYING trucks with Trenton had felt like they were a family. No, Chase didn't know they shared a son, but he'd joined in and played with them as much as his sore ribs would allow. Finally, it ended when Trenton's eyes kept drifting shut and he looked up at her and said, "Watch movie, Mommy."

The three of them curled up on the couch, and watched his favorite show. The moment had been bittersweet, especially when Chase reached over and took her hand and held it in his. Soon sleep overcame her and she laid her head on his shoulder, their bodies touching as all of them napped.

How long could she continue without telling him about Trenton? Yet, she knew he would be beyond mad. So angry that she feared he would file suit against her.

A good lawyer, he had the knowledge to take her to court and fight her for custody and that was her biggest fear. The very thought of someone taking her son was bone crushing. Seeing her baby taken from her arms would devastate her and never happen.

Even if she had to run to keep him with her, she would.

That night, lying in bed with Trenton sleeping next to her, her cell phone beeped. Glancing at the number she recognized Ally's name. Quietly, she answered the call.

"Hang on a minute, let me step outside," she said.

Grabbing a robe, she walked out of the bedroom closing the door behind her. "It's midnight, what's up?"

"I had to warn you," she said. "Keep the doors and windows locked. Roger knows where you are."

"Crap," she said. "That's not what I need now."

These past few days they'd settled into a routine. A nice, ordinary day with everyone doing what they wanted at their own pace. So far, the time spent here was comfortable and right.

"Why do you think he found me?"

"Somehow he pinged your location. While you guys talked, he was able to pinpoint your signal via your phone."

"Oh no, I forgot all about him adding that app to protect me. At the time, he told me he can look on there and locate where I'm at. He said it was for my protection."

"Exactly."

"Yesterday, he came to see me. Just back from Vegas and he's got the divorce proceedings started. And he's coming to see you."

Laney sighed. The man didn't seem to want to give up and she feared this might get ugly.

"Maybe you should come home," Ally said. "Or I should come out there."

Exactly what she didn't need or want. Ally or anyone else to drop in. Ally didn't realize that Chase was here and Roger would be even more angry she wasn't alone.

"No, I'll be fine. I'm not afraid of him and I'll call the law if he decides to come," she said, hoping he wouldn't. Almost certain he would show up at the most inopportune time.

"Promise me, you'll call right after you phone the sheriff. Roger's infuriated, really mad and you don't need to be by yourself with him."

"What's he mad about? He's the one who screwed everything up. We would have been married now if he hadn't tied the knot with his blonde bombshell in Vegas."

At the bachelor party, she expected Roger to have a fun time. Getting completely wasted and finding himself in bed wed to a woman was totally unacceptable. His failure was no longer her problem.

Ally laughed. "Evidently, she thinks she's found herself a meal ticket and she's hanging on like a tick on a deer and going for the ride of her life."

"Maybe what happened fate ordained," Laney said, thinking

about the matchmaker in Bride. "Maybe, just maybe, things happen for a reason and karma decided we didn't belong together."

Nancy believed her and Chase were meant for each other. The secrets between them, she didn't know if they could ever overcome. Yes, she kept their child a secret, but only to let him accomplish his dreams, his goals.

Confronting him in the past, then he wouldn't be the man he was today. Would he accept her explanation and was she inclined to inform him? A shiver went through her, no.

"Sounds like the river is doing you some good. You sound less stressed and rational," Ally said with a laugh. "More like the girl I grew up with."

"Good, I'm not ready to admit this is what I needed, but it has been relaxing and revealing. Even a little scary at times."

Silence on the other end of the phone told Laney she'd frightened her friend. "Like in high water over the bridge kind of scary."

"Oh that," Ally said. "Didn't you hear me yelling at you?"

"No, you didn't," Laney said.

"Just as I started to tell you about the bridge, you ran out the door of the church."

"I learned about the high water from firsthand experience. As soon as we arrived, I chan--" she couldn't tell her that Chase kicked them out because then she would find out he was here.

"Anyway, we tried to leave to go to the store and the river was out of its banks. I almost drove off into it. Thank goodness, I stopped when I did."

Laney didn't like to lie, but she couldn't tell Ally the real story. Someday, but not now.

Again, silence, before Ally finally responded. "I'm sorry, Laney. In my life, that's only happened three or four times, but I heard they were forecasting heavy rain and should have warned you. But I don't like to talk to you in the car when Trenton is with you."

A nurse, Ally had seen too many small children hurt in car accidents while the parent chatted on the phone when driving. She refused to contribute to the injury of a child if she could help it. Whenever Laney told her she was in the car, she hung up.

"Anyway, I wanted to tell you that Roger will probably show up. Don't be surprised if he does tomorrow, Friday night."

"Thanks for warning me, but he's wasting his time if he comes out here. There's no going back. What's done is done and I'm moving on."

Literally, she was moving on. The image of Chase came to mind and things between them were changing for the better. Right up until he learned the truth about her son.

STRIP POKER...OH my goodness, they played the most watered down version of this game he'd ever experienced. They started off playing Spit - a card game of speed and wit, but quickly realized the noise might wake up Trenton.

Then they decided to play strip poker...but Laney refused to shed her clothes. Wearing only her swimsuit and cover-up, they would be naked in no time. So, if you lost you had to do something silly or ridiculous that was decided on before the beginning of the hand.

"Let's change this up a bit," he said. "If I win, you must tell me what happened the night I took you home at six o'clock in the morning."

As she dealt the cards, she smiled and said, "We've spoken very little about that night."

"Agreed," he said, picking up his cards staring in wonder at the three aces. "After the night in the woods, I went on vacation and when I came back, I didn't see you until right before I left."

"Oh, yes, you promised to call me and never did," she said.

What could he say? That summer he spent his time lining up everything to attend law school and enjoying his free time celebrating his graduation from college.

Looking at her made him forget everything he wanted in his life and left him reeling with need for her. It had been that way years ago. Now, it was worse.

At least now he was a man, not someone heading off to finish his schooling. Now, he had his career on the right path, everything under control, except for his ex-girlfriend. And she was gone.

With a shrug, he said, "You're right. I'm not stupid and I perceived you were perilous."

"Huh?" she said, gazing at him.

"Threatening, as in, if I called you, we would start dating. Then I would sleep with you again and maybe this time, I couldn't leave you behind. Maybe a second or third date, we would find a preacher and get married. After that, you terrified me, so I ran as fast as I could toward school."

Holding her cards in her hand, she gaped at him. Finally, she closed her mouth and laid her cards down. "All you had to do was tell me."

"What? That a small brunette frightened me. The night we stayed together in the woods was the best sex of my life? Being with you made me think of dumping my goals and grabbing you and running? What kind of man do you think I am?"

To admit that to a woman while in his twenties was impossible. Those words made him vulnerable and needy, and yes, he wanted her in the worst possible way.

"Yes, you should have told me."

"What would that have accomplished?" he asked. "Both of us were still in school, where we needed to be."

"Instead you left me broken hearted. That night stirred up so many feelings and then you never called and you just drove off, leaving me standing in the middle of the road. For the last four years, I've thought you were an asshat."

When he left, she was broken hearted? Never before had he considered how his departure affected her. Or if she cared enough about him.

"A what?"

"You know, someone with their head up their..."

A smile turned up his lips as he stared at Laney. Even after running from her, she'd never been far from his mind and sometimes he tried to keep from seeing her when he came home.

"Oh, now I know what you mean. Because I walked away, my head is up my derrière."

"Couldn't have said it better."

Throwing down his cards, he laughed and grabbed her by the arm, pulling her close.

"You're right. After one night, I thought here was a woman who had the ability to twist me in knots. I wasn't mentally or emotionally prepared for what you did to me. And it takes a mighty strong man to confess to those weaknesses. Now I'm older and wiser and so much more qualified. So, bring it on."

His head dipped, his lips claiming hers in a kiss that spun him around. No matter how much he primed for the assault on his emotions, her kiss twisted and turned and churned his gut into a mess of trembling need. A need for him to sacrifice everything to be in her arms once again.

Pushing her down on the sofa, his mouth never left hers as his tongue slipped between her lips, crushing her chest against his as much as he could stand. He wanted to feel her closer, he wanted to taste her from her head to her toes and back up. He wanted to hear her cry when she came apart in his arms. And he wanted it now.

Headlights flashed and the sound of a vehicle coming up the

drive had them separating. The engine stopped and they glanced out the window.

"Someone's here."

"Laney," a man yelled.

"Crap, it's Roger," she said pushing him away and rising. "This is not going to be pretty."

CHAPTER 10

*L*aney was fighting mad. How dare Roger find her when she told him countless times they were done. Yanking open the door, she walked outside onto the porch.

"We need to talk."

She didn't want him in the house. She didn't want him to find Chase here or it would be all over the town of Cupid and probably Bride, as well, before the sun rose.

"How dare you show up here. Everything has been said. It's over."

"Please, you haven't given me a moment to explain what happened."

"Did you have sex with that woman?" At first, she thought that was the reason for their break-up, but now she knew there were other factors. Major ones. Thankfully, she learned they didn't have the right kind of love to be together.

Roger rubbed his hand over his eyes, like he couldn't believe she didn't want him here.

"Turn your truck around and go home. We're done."

"Give me a chance," he called.

"There is nothing more to say," she said.

"I love you."

No matter how hard or how bad her next words sounded, she had to be truthful and honest with him. The time had come and gone for them. Thankfully, the relationship ended before she took the final vow.

"If you loved me, you wouldn't have cheated."

"I'm asking you to forgive me," he said. "Give us a second chance."

She stepped farther away from the house, not wanting his yelling to wake up Trenton. Her son didn't need to witness this kind of drama. Even she didn't want to be a part of it, but sometimes you had to take a fire extinguisher to a blaze. Right now, Roger was an inferno. Time to extinguish the burn.

"You're forgiven, but I'm not marrying you. After everything happened, I realized my love for you is not the forever kind, but more the brotherly affection. Roger, I care about you, but not enough to spend the rest of my life at your side as your wife. So, I'm trying to let you down easy, but this is over."

At that moment, Chase stepped out the door and Roger's face contorted into an ugly growling beast as he charged him. "You son of a bit..."

Roger slammed into Chase, who doubled up his fist and swung, knocking him to the ground.

A cracking noise and the spurt of blood shocked the two men.

Pushing between them. "Stop or I'm calling the sheriff."

"A man I don't know took my woman and he broke my nose," Roger cried.

"Oh, please, I'm not your woman. And you charged him," Laney responded, thinking she had never seen Roger act this way.

Had she not known him or could this be the response of a desperate man. Dropping her timbre in her best stern teacher's voice like she was dealing with an unruly student she stood over him.

"Enough. Roger, you have two choices. Leave here now and never return or I call the law. Nothing you say will bring us back together. Which do you choose?"

"I'll go. But I'm surprised to find you here with another man, cheating on me?"

"Don't even go there. Really, you can say that to me," she said in a huff. The man was a complete hypocrite. The only reason she was giving him an explanation was because she wanted no doubt in his mind she would ever cheat.

"What does it matter to you? Both of us arrived at the cabin at the same time. Chase and I are friends, nothing more," she said softly.

Were they? Though she hated Chase at first, now she no longer felt that way. With sudden realization, she wanted to explore this new relationship growing between her and Chase.

Time to step away and breathe. Time to bring everything back under control before there was more violence.

"Let me get you a bag of ice and some paper towels. Then you need to go," she said.

In a few minutes, she returned and watched as the man she thought she loved and had planned on marrying slowly walked back to his truck. A heavy burden lifted from her chest. Finally, maybe, he understood it was over.

Turning toward Chase, she went to him. "How are you feeling?"

"Like someone put a target on my back. Another altercation. Why am I getting in all these brawls?" He threw his hands up and then grimaced. "In my life, I fight with words, not my fists and yet here I am once again slugging it out."

Lifting his hand, she gazed at his scraped knuckles and then raised it to her lips kissing each knuckle. "Thank you for protecting me."

"Oh, a little more to the left," he said with a sigh.

Of course, he was taking advantage of the situation, but she liked his teasing manner. Seeing him safe guard her filled her with pride.

Letting her mouth slide across the back of his hand. "Thank you for defending me."

"Aww, a little more," he whispered.

Flipping his hand over she kissed the inside of his palm and let her tongue swipe over the skin. He sighed and closed his eyes.

"Do that again," he moaned.

So she did.

"Aww, if only my ribs would stop screaming in protest," he said with a painful whine.

Placing her arm around him, barely touching his rib area, she could see he was worn out. "Come on, let me help you back on the couch with the ice pack and I'll bring you a pain pill."

"I'd rather you tucked me in bed," he said low in her ear.

Leaning in, she kissed his neck. "As long as you don't expect anything else."

"If my ribs weren't sore, you would find it hard to resist my case." Chase groaned. "This is not fair. I've been the protector of women and animals and I'm the one suffering. Not the yahoos who created all this drama."

"Too bad, but you also get brownie points for protecting me."

Laying his head on her shoulder, he said, "At least, I'm getting brownie points. Now tuck me in bed before I collapse."

TWO DAYS LATER, Laney felt like a dump truck had been removed from her chest. Roger no longer held her back and she enjoyed Chase's company so much more than when she first arrived. No longer did she want to strangle him for his part in her duplicity.

In fact, now that she could look back on those days, she realized if she'd told him about the pregnancy, his dream would have died right there in the driveway. She couldn't do that to him.

How did she go about telling him now? Was she ready to let him know that Trenton was his son?

After being cooped up in the house for the last few days, they decided going out to dinner would be a great excuse to leave the cabin. Trenton had pizza several days ago, so they chose to stop at the Stable, a country western restaurant famous for its fries.

At nine o'clock they cleared the dining area of all families and opened the dance floor to everyone. Before then, it was a family joint.

Being escorted to their table, Laney noticed the signed photos of country and western stars on the wall. Some celebrities had eaten at the bar and all the autographs mentioned their delicious fries.

"Momma, cowboys," Trenton said, glancing at a group of men sitting at a table. They were all decked out in jeans and boots and button-down shirts.

"Yes, son," she said, wondering if they were the real ones who worked on a nearby ranch of the dressed-up store variety.

Chase's hand at her back gently guided her to the table. A tingle of awareness spiraled down her spine at the warmth his touch generated on her back. The man could still make her feel like that twenty-year-old college student responding to a dare that almost got her arrested.

"Okay, folks, here you go. Your waitress will be right out. Enjoy your meal," the hostess in shorts and boots said to them as they were seated.

As she stared at the young woman thinking about her carefree life, Laney knew the hostess must consider her old, but couldn't imagine living without Trenton. Even without a man, she wouldn't trade her life for anything. Looking over, she made certain Trenton was strapped into his chair.

The waitress came to take their order, she looked up at her. "Can you tell me about your fries?"

"Fried potatoes covered in cheese with peppers or plain, your choice."

"What kind of oil do you fry your potatoes in? My son is allergic to coconut oil, so I always check."

Chase's head jerked up from the menu he was scanning, his brown eyes widened as he stared at her. "Trenton is allergic to coconut oil? I'm also allergic."

Panic like a vise around her neck squeezed and she lifted her glass of water, trying to ease the pain. Gulping down the drink, gave her a moment to gather a logical response that didn't take him down the path she feared the most.

Setting the water down, she cleared her throat. "Ugh, I think I swallowed a bug."

His eyes darkened as he gazed at her. "Maybe, but I didn't see anything flying around."

"My throat closed up for a second," she said. "It's better now."

The cute little girl glanced between the two of them oddly. "Let me ask the kitchen."

"How weird that we share the same allergies," Chase said, a frown gathering on his forehead.

"Yes, coconut allergies are rather rare. Are you also allergic to tree nuts as well? Most people are allergic to both," she said, trying her best to stay away from the elephant in the room.

Regardless, she would never risk Trenton's health, so whenever they had fried food, she asked. Those first few times he had a reaction scared her plenty. If possible, she didn't want to ever witness him so violently ill again.

Chase studied her son, making her skittish. This restaurant was not the place to tell him about Trenton.

Finally, he turned and contemplated her, a puzzled expression on his face, his mind swirling. "Yes, I'm allergic to all kinds of nuts except for peanuts. Those I can have, but not almonds or hazelnuts or any of the ones I enjoy. But I don't stop breathing, I just get sick and my skin reacts. Is that how his allergy presents?"

That was exactly what happened to Trenton. Every time she gave him a sip of her coconut water, he became ill and hives would break out on his skin. Then when she gave him a taste of pure coconut the poor baby had suffered for two days. After that she avoided coconut. Since then no reactions.

She swallowed, wishing she could avoid this question. "He breaks out in hives and becomes very sick."

The server came back. "The potatoes are fried in canola oil."

"Okay, we'll have a large order," Chase said. "Could you bring the peppers on the side. I don't think the young man here is ready for jalapeños."

Reaching over, he brushed Trenton's hair out of his face.

"Truck, Momma, truck."

Opening her bag, she handed her son, his tiny truck. "Here you go."

"Mom always told me when I was his age, I liked to play with trucks," Chase said, looking back at Laney.

How had they gone from a peaceful dinner to one that made her more nervous than the fateful day she walked down the aisle. "Don't all boys like toy cars and trucks."

"And girls," he said, gazing at her. "How old were you when I picked you up dancing around the Cupid statue?"

A ball of fear of gathered in the pit of her stomach. Was he doing the numbers in his head? Should she lie? No, the time for lies was all past. The truth would set you free or some other trite saying. "That summer, I just turned twenty and was about to enter my second year of college."

Instead, she took classes online right up until the day she delivered.

"So, I'm about four years older than you. How did you continue going to school with a small child?"

Those days had been hard. Especially at first when he was so small. Born in April, she barely passed her final exams that semester dealing with the birth of a baby and being a single, new mother.

"My mother took care of him during the day while I attended class. When I came home, I fed him, bathed him and rocked him to sleep before I did my homework. Without my parents help, I never would have completed my schooling."

With a quick glance at Trenton, her chest tightened and overflowed with love for the tyke. There was no doubt, she would do it all over again. "We made it through and I finished a year ago."

"Almost the same time I graduated from law school."

"Yes," she said, remembering Ally talking about attending her brother's graduation.

"Do you like teaching?" he asked.

At the thought of her students, she smiled. "The kids are the best. Working with the administration is frustrating, but I wouldn't give it up. How about you? Do you love being a lawyer?"

On purpose, she diverted the conversation to him, trying to change the focus from herself and Trenton's birth. Learning he was allergic to coconut set off his alarms and she could see his mind churning over that fact about the two of them, creating a burning ball of fear in her stomach. By no means was Chase a stupid man.

Nodding, his lips pressed together. "For me, I love the drama of the courtroom. Fighting to prove someone innocent or getting a mother the child support her baby needs or fighting an unjust system for someone. Those things I enjoy about being an attorney. Doing wills, writing letters..." he yawned. "A complete bore. My life is good and I'm happy. It would be better if I had a steady partner, but so far that hasn't happened."

Suddenly he softened as he grabbed her hand and brought it to his mouth. "Maybe that's about to change."

Her stomach clenched as she stared into his dark brown eyes, the color of Trenton's. Wasn't this what she wanted? Wasn't he the man who she dreamed about, but how did she tell him Trenton was his son?

$$\text{⚓}$$

ON THE TRIP HOME, Trenton fell asleep in his car seat. Parking the truck, Laney reached for him and Chase stopped her. "Let me carry him in."

The sleepy little boy didn't move as he lifted his limp body and carried him inside the house. The sweet child smell wafted over him, his little arms looped around his neck, sending his brain into overdrive.

Never before had he considered the boy might be his. Tonight, when she mentioned his allergy to coconut, the fact Trenton might be his son slammed him like a fist to the face. Why did he never consider the obvious?

Only one night they shared their bodies, their souls. One wonderful night and they used protection, being careful not to take the risk of a child. Never did he have sex with anyone without using a condom. But if Trenton was his boy, why didn't she tell him about the pregnancy. Why did she lie?

"Just carry him into the bedroom and I'll put him to bed," she said quietly.

If this boy was his son, she would have some explaining to do.

He laid the boy he'd grown fond of on the bed and the tyke promptly rolled over. Observing, Laney removing his shoes and socks he couldn't help but think of the time lost watching him grow. Could Trenton be his?

At that moment, he made a vow he wouldn't miss another moment. First, he had to know for certain and he had a DNA test in his room that he bought with the sole purpose of finding Trenton's father. When he purchased the kit, he never imagined he would use it on himself, because he had no clue the child was his.

"Look, it's late and I'm going to turn in."

"Yeah, me, too," he lied, knowing the person he should call to help answer questions like if Trenton was his son or not. His mother.

Giving her a quick peck on the lips instead of the steamier ones they experienced lately, he needed time to think. Those passionate kisses had him dreaming of their night together and wanting to experience that same desire once again.

Walking out of the room, when he reached the door he glanced back. No, he couldn't be his son. Laney would never hurt him that way.

Hurrying down the hall, he went into his room and picked up his phone and dialed his mother.

"Hey, Mom," he said, knowing she would give him shit for not having called lately.

"I was beginning to get worried about you," she said. "It's been weeks since you've called. What is going on?"

"Oh, I've been involved in a big case," he lied, the boy inside him squirming. If he told her the truth, she'd be here before the sun rose over the horizon to check on him and also to examine Trenton.

For the next five minutes, they chit-chatted about the family and she told him all about Ally being a bridesmaid at Laney's disastrous wedding. Chase listened, wishing he could talk to her about the situation, but knowing he couldn't.

Since graduating from college, his mother longed for grandchildren and if she learned there was a possibility, the road would burn up beneath the tires of her car.

"Mom, I have a question for you. When I was a baby, when did you learn I was allergic to coconut?"

"Oh, dear," she said. "I'll never forget the first time I gave you some coconut pudding when you were small, maybe two or three. That little bowl of custard made you so ill. The first time, I didn't fathom why you were sick. The second time, I quickly realized the problem and from then on, absolutely no coconut in our home."

Silent, he thought about Trenton's allergies. They were like his own.

"Why do you ask?" she said.

"Oh, a friend of mine, her child reacts to coconut and I wondered how you learned about the allergy."

"In less than an hour, you broke out in hives," she said.

Laney mentioned Trenton would get hives.

"Well, that's good to know," he said. They continued talking for another five minutes before he ended the call. So, Trenton reacted to coconut the same way he did.

Picking up the box that held the DNA test, he read the instructions carefully. Then he took out the swabs and following instructions, he swabbed the inside of his mouth and put it in the bottle.

Tomorrow, when Laney wasn't around, he would swab Trenton's cheek. And soon after, he would learn the truth. Was Trenton his son?

$\mathcal{T}$he next morning while Laney cooked breakfast, Chase swabbed Trenton's mouth.

"Bad," Trenton called shaking his head.

Turning around to gaze at him sitting in his chair at the table, she asked, "What's bad?"

"Pulled a piece of paper towel out of his mouth," Chase said, sliding the swab into the container before she saw it. Yes, it was lying. Yes, he felt bad about concealing this test from Laney. But she would never agree to a DNA test and what if the boy was his son? Then, he had every right to know. That justified his actions.

"Oh, that's weird," she said, flipping the eggs.

"Why don't we go fishing after breakfast," Chase said, needing to escape the confines of the house. Away from the walls pressing in on him. Since yesterday, a sense of being deceived over-whelmed him. Cornered by the knowledge he suspected she was hiding from him.

After they talked last night, he did the math, counting nine months and would be shocked if Trenton's DNA didn't match his own. In some ways, he wanted the child to be his. More than anything, he wanted the child's mother. Spending time together, the attraction he feared so many years ago now raged through him.

Only now, she was a robust, spirited, independent, beautiful woman. And he was having a hard time keeping his hands off her.

Yet, was it feasible for him to ever forgive her for the time he missed watching the boy grow up if Trenton was his son. The possibility of him having both of them was better if Trenton was not. Because when he learned the truth, depending on the answer, he would be happy or furious or maybe both.

"Fishing," Trenton yelled. "Fishing."

"You don't even know what fishing is," she said gazing at her son.

"Uh, huh. Pops took me fishing," he said. "Put worm on a hook and wait for fish to bite."

Chase chuckled and gave the kid a fist bump. Seemed like a simple enough explanation. The kid was smart and definitely a child to be watched at all times. One little slip and he could be in the water.

Still, getting out of the house would help him stop thinking about the possibilities and it would be a fun outing for them all.

"Your mother can't fish, that's the problem," he said quietly. "Tell her this is men's work."

The child laughed and pushed out his chest. Amazing, at this age, already the boy recognized the difference in the roles of men and women. "Momma, you don't know how to fish."

Rotating from the stove, she tossed a glance at the two of them. "Ha, we'll see who catches the first one."

"No, me, Momma. I'm going to catch the biggest one."

With a shake of her head, she gave him an exasperated look. "See what you've started. Looks like today we're going fishing."

Trenton and Chase laughed. "Don't worry, I got you, buddy. We'll beat her."

After they ate, they loaded up their gear and headed down to the river. The water had receded some, but still moved swifter than normal and Chase had a moment of unease. They would have to keep a close eye on Trenton.

"Here, Trenton," he said, kneeling and putting a life jacket on the boy.

"Don't want to wear this," Trenton whined.

"Then we're going back to the house," Laney told him. "This is your choice. Fish with a life jacket on or we go back to the house."

The child stuck his lip out in a pout, but didn't whine anymore. Chase knew they would both guard him carefully, but in case Trenton fell in, at least he would be a little safer. Chase's ribs were still sore from the bike accident and he wouldn't last long in the rapidly moving water, but he would die trying to rescue a small child.

"Let's get your pole ready," Chase said as he slipped the bait on the hook while Trenton jumped up and down.

"Me put in water."

The boy couldn't throw it out far enough, but maybe he would let Chase help him toss out the line.

Walking over, Laney gazed at the two of them. "Do you need some help?"

"No, we've got this," Chase told her. "Better put your line in the water if you're going to beat us because. We're ready."

"Well, if I'm not needed," she said and walked away.

Reaching out, he took her by the hand. "You're needed."

Staring at her, his heart swelled, though an undercurrent of suspicion caused him to doubt his emotions. Still, the urge to kiss her was strong, but a little boy stood between them watching everything going on looking up to see what they were doing. Not the time.

A soft smile crossed her face, the promise of kissing, later. Lots of kissing and more if possible.

"Come on, Trenton, let's catch our first fish," he said, taking the boy by the hand and leading him near the water's edge. "This is as close as you get to the water. Do you understand?"

"Yes," the child said, jumping up and down. "Let me. Let me."

Holding onto the back of Trenton's life jacket, the kid tried to cast the line out, but it dropped down in front of them.

"What if we do it together," Chase suggested.

"Okay," the boy said.

As soon as their line was out, he pulled over a lawn chair and pulled Trenton onto his lap. "Now, we wait."

"Come on, fishie, bite my worm," the boy called. "They're going to take a bite, we'll pull them in and cook them for supper."

Chase never realized how enjoyable kids could be, but he also understood they were a lot of responsibility and work as well. Even now, he had no doubts he would welcome all of the challenges that came with parenting.

Looking at Laney, he watched as the wind teased her hair and her bobber went under.

"Oh, I've got a bite," she said and yanked on the line. For a second, he thought she had it, but at the top of the water, the crappie jerked its head enough to pull the hook loose.

"Drat," she said. "My plan was to show you guys a woman can fish."

Just then their bobber went under. "Fish," Trenton cried.

"Reel it in," he told the young boy as he held up the rod, keeping tension on the line as the child cranked the wheel. Together the two of them managed to land a small crappie.

"Look, Mommy, look. I caught fish."

"Oh my, you're the big winner. Now get another one."

For the next hour, they pulled in a total of five crappie to Laney's meager two. Finally, Trenton began to tire and they decided to go in.

"Time to go, so reel in your line," he told Trenton.

"Okay," he responded. Chase was amazed at how the kid

didn't lose interest and genuinely enjoyed watching his bobber for any movement.

The three of them always had fun together. The atmosphere natural and easy going, like they were meant to be together. Like they were a family.

After a couple of minutes, Trenton handed the pole to Chase. "Ready for movie."

Chase turned to look at Laney and heard her make a strange strangled noise. In disbelief, he stared as the earth beneath her feet crumbled and she tumbled into the river.

"Laney," he screamed.

The swift moving water pulled her and she tried to swim back to the bank, but the river wasn't done with her and it tossed her like a doll farther down the shoreline.

He started to jump in and then glanced at Trenton. Somehow, he had to save her.

Leaning down to Trenton, he took him by the shoulders. "Don't move. Stay right here."

"Mommy?"

"I'm going to help her," he said.

In the churning, boiling water, the current dragged her downstream. Racing along the river, never losing sight of her, he searched for a calm expanse where she could swim to shore.

Running beside the stream, a long, broken limb almost tripped him and he wondered if there was a way to use it as a lifeline. Picking it up, he discovered the wood was only five inches thick, but still green enough that it might hold and not break when he pulled.

"Laney," he continued to yell, letting her know he was following her. If the water calmed, he would dive in and somehow bring her back to the bank.

Her head bobbed in the water as she tried to paddle toward the shore, but the swiftly moving current refused to let her go. If only he had a rope, but he didn't have time to run back to the house. Glancing back, he saw Trenton standing there crying. Thank goodness, the boy was doing exactly like he said and not moving.

He ran like a sixteen-year-old track star, but still he couldn't catch up with her. Until she slammed against a large rock jutting up out of the river. Breathing hard, his chest aching with fear, he finally stood across from her.

"Hang on," he shouted.

Lying on the muddy edge, he extended the branch to her. While his ribs screamed in protest, he stretched until she grabbed on. With his heart pounding hard, hanging on tightly to the limb, he pulled her toward the bank, praying her grip held. Even with the water tugging at her, she clasped the limb.

With the last bit of his strength, he grabbed her, hauling her up out of the river and into his arms. Trembling, she started to sob while he held her snug against him like he never wanted to let her go.

"That was so scary."

"Yes," he said. "We're lucky I found that limb, because I didn't know how to save you."

Nodding her head, she sighed against his chest.

"Where's Trenton?"

"Back with the supplies. I told him not to move and then came after you," he said.

Taking a deep breath, she released it slowly, though her hands shook like an agitator in a washing machine. "Come on, let's hurry back to him."

Coming over the ridge as they walked up the embankment, Trenton stood in the same spot, sniffling. Chase gasped with relief that the child had grasped the danger and stayed where he was at.

"Baby," she called and he came running to her, his short little legs going as fast as he could.

Trenton ran into her arms. "Momma, you okay."

Chase observed as she held Trenton tightly, hugging him as tears flowed from her eyes, she tried to contain the sobs. What would have happened to this little boy if she'd drowned. Chase had to turn away, seeing the emotional reunion of the boy and his mother.

"You're squeezing too hard," Trenton managed.

She freed him and he leaned back and ran his finger down her cheek, drying her tears. "Don't cry, Mommy. Chase saved you."

"Yes, he did, baby. Now do you understand why I didn't want you to fall into the river."

"Bad water," Trenton said. "Bad."

"Yes, baby, it was bad. Maybe we should go back to the house and have some lunch," she said.

"Hungry," the little boy said.

Rising slowly, Laney's gaze looked almost haunted. All he could think was he almost lost her and they hadn't even really had a chance. Why did it feel like something loomed over him that he should realize? Grasping her hand, he stared into her shamrock-green eyes, so grateful they still were vibrant with life.

"Come on. Fishing has lost its appeal," he said and took Trenton by the hand. "A ham sandwich sounds wonderful."

Fixated on her emerald eyes, he wanted to lose himself in her arms and hold her like he'd never let her go.

"Starving," he said, but knew food wouldn't satisfy his craving.

At the touch of her hand in his, he swallowed hard, pushing down the emotion that clogged his throat. Today, could have ended so much worse.

Stunned, at the intense emotions flooding his senses, he accepted he was falling in love with Laney. After all these years, he knew he loved her and longed to make a life with her.

WHEN THEY REACHED THE HOUSE, Laney went into the bedroom and completely stripped off her dripping clothes. Still shaking, she sat on the bed and placed her head in her hands and thanked God for sparing her life.

Today, she could have easily drowned. And knew, if not for aiming her body for that rock, the current would've continued to hurl her down the river until her struggles ended along with her life.

At this moment, she wasn't ready to die. She had a little boy to protect and help grow into a young man. Eventually she wanted more children and a husband. Together, she dreamed of creating their own family. There was so much to look forward to in this life and she was wasting time.

Chase's face swam before her teary eyes and she realized she hungered for the chance to explore a relationship with him. To learn if this growing attraction was something they could build a life on.

"Momma, Chase made us lunch," Trenton called.

"Give me just a little time," she answered, needing a few more minutes to herself.

What if she'd been alone? What would happen to Trenton if she died? How would Chase have reacted to her death?

The poor man's face looked deathly white, his expression stark with tension when he held out that branch. Fear kept her clinging to that rock, yet she had to let go and take a chance on a broken limb to help her safely return to the shore. Thank God, it worked.

Maybe after today, she needed to take a chance on Chase.

Today's accident reinforced the fact she wanted to live, to watch her son mature, to reach out and touch a man sleeping in her bed and know she loved him and trusted him with her life. Could that man be Chase?

A knock sounded at the door.

"Laney," he called. "Are you all right?"

She sat nude on the bed trying to get her crap together before she faced the two of them again. Reaching up, she touched the necklace at her throat and wondered, again, who had sent her their heart.

"I'm okay. I just needed a few minutes to change clothes," she said.

Chase opened the door and she grabbed the towel, holding it up against her body, wrapping it around her.

"Nice towel," he said. "Sorry, I had to make certain you were all right."

"Exhausted, drained, shook-up, but I'm grateful to be alive," she said.

Coming into the room, he reached out and brushed her wet hair from her face. "Trenton is sitting at the table, eating his sandwich. Come, join us."

He was standing so close to her, his manly scent comforted her. "Of course, I will. I wanted some time to regroup."

Suddenly he wrapped his arms around her and pulled her in tightly. "You scared me."

"Didn't do much for me, either."

Leaning back, his lips softly grazed hers.

"Mommy," Trenton called.

"He's worried about you," he said. "I'll leave you so you can dress. Don't be too long. I need you as much as he does," he said.

Releasing her, he walked out the door.

Her chest tightened at his words, her heart near bursting. In the last ten days, she felt more for Chase than she ever experienced with anyone.

Hurriedly, she threw clothes on, eager to be with her son, but even more with Chase.

&

LATER THAT EVENING, after she put Trenton down, she glanced

through the glass doors and watched Chase pacing in front of the hot tub in his swim trunks - a bottle of wine sitting on the table.

As he walked back and forth, she swallowed hard. The urge to go to him, comfort him, and ease the tension in his face was strong. The flashback of how many times he'd rescued her, overwhelming. First, when she ran the Cupid dance, then when Roger came, and today when she fell into the river.

If it hadn't been for his quick thinking, she would have died and what would have happened to Trenton?

Sure, her parents would have raised him, but not like his mother, and they were older. They were aging, and this was their time in life to enjoy. Not be burdened with a small growing child, though she knew they loved him.

Staring at Chase, there were things left unsaid between them, but tonight she needed to feel his arms around her and lie in the safe sanctuary of his arms. In a hurry, she dashed into the bedroom, careful not to wake her son and slipped on her bathing suit. Though, you would think more water was not what she needed, she wanted this evening with Chase.

In a few moments, she walked out onto the patio. Halting his frantic steps, his head jerked up and he gazed at her.

"After a day like today, we both deserved a soak in the tub with an alcoholic beverage," he said his eyes darkening at the sight of her.

"Great idea," she agreed.

Removing the cork from the bottle, she jumped at the loud pop. Automatically, her hand reached up to touch the golden heart necklace around her neck.

"Tonight, we deserve a little relaxation," he said as he handed her a wine glass. Grabbing her by the hand, he helped her into the hot tub.

The water rushed over her legs, and for a moment, she felt panic, recalling the horror from today rushing through her. Taking a deep breath, she slowly released the fear and the apprehension. Today's accident would not overshadow her life, regardless that it scared her plenty.

"Is it too hot," he asked, gazing at her concern reflecting from his eyes.

"No, just a memory from today," she said forcing herself to sink into the water.

"Ah," he said and sat beside her, wrapping his arm around her. "Here we are, riding the rapids together. Hang on, we're coming into white water."

Laughing, he pulled them up and down, splashing in the hot tub. A giggle escaped her. "You're being silly."

"I'm trying to recreate your experience today and end it on a better note," he said, sipping his drink. "Luck had me almost tripping over the branch lying on the bank. At the time, I thought this might help me, but I wasn't certain the limb was strong enough. Thank God, it worked."

Her chest tightened and she could feel tears welling up in her eyes and she quickly blinked them away. Somehow she survived, though it would be awhile before she went fishing again.

With a yank, he gruffly pulled her in close, his voice rough with emotion. "When I shut my eyes, the terror of those first few minutes slams into my gut and I'm panicked Trenton could be deprived of his mom. And I'm afraid the boy will not stay where I told him. The thought of him falling in the water, while I saved you was very frightening. But more importantly, I'm terrified I'll lose the woman I care deeply for."

Leaning down, he kissed her, his lips covering hers, sealing their mouths together like he never wanted to let her go and she didn't want him to stop. Finally, she pushed back.

Now was the time she should tell him about Trenton. Now she should confess the day he left for law school, she had come to tell him they were expecting a baby. But then the night would be ruined and she didn't want it to end with them at odds.

This night was theirs and she wanted it in such a bad way that she was willing to risk everything. Even another baby. Tomorrow she would tell him.

Rising from the water, she looked down at him. "I've had enough water for one day. Enough wine, but what I really want is to spend the night in your arms, clinging to and being comforted by you."

His eyes widened in disbelief and she smiled and held out her hand, which he quickly grabbed.

"There is nothing I would rather do," he said, stepping out of the hot tub, turning and lifting her into his arms.

CHAPTER 12

*L*aney woke early that morning with a start, in Chase's bed. For a moment, she lay beside the man, her chest pounding out of control, with fear coursing through her veins, almost panicking. What the hell had she done?

Last night had been perfect, even better than the night they spent lost in the woods, but still she was a grown woman with a child in the next room. Chase could use it against her in a court of law if he decided to try to gain custody of Trenton.

Glancing at him, tears built in her eyes, her chest ached and she stuffed her hand in her mouth to silence her cries. She loved him, probably since that night he rescued her in Cupid and soothed her when they were wandering in the dark where he reassured a young woman and comforted her. Then yesterday, she owed her life to him.

Once again, she willingly gave him her heart and soul and now she feared he would take her boy.

Chase was not dumb and sooner or later, he would demand some answers on Trenton. When he learned Trenton was his son, he would be furious.

The best thing she could do to keep Trenton's identity safe

was to leave now before Chase started doing the math and realizing she deliberately kept the truth from him.

Maybe she'd been wrong not to stand up to him that day, other than let him walk away to fulfill his dreams, but she knew how much he wanted to be a lawyer and supporting a wife and child would not have helped him reach his goals.

They would always be tied together because they shared a child, but couldn't tell him now because she suspected he would use his skills to obtain the son she loved.

Rising slowly to not awaken the man, she chose the path that it seemed she always took, putting her son's life above her own needs. Choosing his safety and happiness.

At the door, she reached up and touched the gold heart necklace at her throat, gazed at Chase, and realized no other man would ever have her heart. No man would ever take his place and that's what hurt most of all. She loved Chase, but would never let him take her son. After all these years, she was still paying for that choice years ago.

CHASE SLOWLY OPENED his eyes and reached across the bed looking for the woman who not only fulfilled his dreams as a young man, but even more as an adult. Spending the night in her arms had seemed life changing.

Several times she mentioned him leaving for law school. That must have hurt her when he abruptly left without calling her. In his gut, he knew they were intended to spend their life together. Even then, he refused to face that fact.

Suddenly he realized someone pounded on the door.

Jumping out of bed, he reached for sweat pants and pulled them over his naked body. Why were no noises coming from the kitchen? Upon awakening, he felt certain she was cooking breakfast, but there was no sound, but the pounding on the door. Did she get locked out?

Walking out of the bedroom, he glanced back at the bed. Did last night really happen or was it a recurring dream. No, he remembered every moment in Laney's arms.

Hurrying toward the knocking he heard, he flung open the door surprised to see Ally, his sister standing there.

"Why are you here?" she said, walking in.

"What happened to your key?" he asked.

"Gave it to Laney. On the spur of the moment, I decided to come spend the weekend with the two of them. Try to cheer her up. Where is she?"

As he looked around the living room, he noticed all of Trenton's toys were gone. His favorite truck, his movies, even the bear he slept with were missing. Like a tomb, silence filled the house with no sounds of a little boy's giggles or his mother chasing after him.

Running his hand through his hair, he gazed at his sister not knowing how to answer her, an overwhelming sense of sadness flowing through him. Obviously, sometime during the night, she'd taken off.

"I don't know. She's been here," he said, standing in the middle of the room feeling like someone just kicked his sore ribs and knocked the breath from him.

Ally stared at him and then she walked through the house to the spare room to check for her friend. When she came back, she strolled into the kitchen.

Picking up a piece of paper laying on the counter that he hadn't seen, she began to read out loud.

"Dear Chase,

The time spent with you these last two weeks has been healing, but I needed to get back to Cupid and put Trenton back on a regular schedule. Last night was very special and it was great to reconnect with you after all these years. Maybe we'll see each other around. Since we are both trying to heal, I fear last night might have been a mistake. Thanks for sharing the cabin with me and Trenton. Yours, Laney."

Ally looked up from the note, her eyes widened and she glared at him. "Oh my, you slept with her," she said, her eyes wide, her voice trembling. "How could you take advantage of my friend? You big jerk!"

"Hey, it was mutual."

"Still, she was vulnerable. Come on, she's had a tough time lately," Ally defended. "And you used her weakness and had sex with her. This is an example of the full Laney defense mode and she's running so fast, you may never catch her. How could you sleep with her at the most defenseless time in her life?"

Striding over to the coffee pot, he needed caffeine to deal with an irate sister. Like a fist, his heart clenched in his chest, shattering like someone smacked a blow whacking the air from his lungs. Why did she leave? What hurt the worst was her total nonchalant attitude about last night. Had their lovemaking meant nothing to her.

Last night, he fell asleep after the best lovemaking of his life with her in his arms. Last night, he all but told her he loved her, wanting to wait until he could somehow make it memorable. Like *on one knee with a ring* memorable.

Instead, he awakened to his sister pounding on the door, and an empty bed.

Last night, when he thought everything between them appeared remarkable, had he been dreaming?

"Have you ever considered for one moment that she did me wrong? Drifting off to sleep, she implied everything was fine and now I wake up with you at my door and she's gone."

Like a bolt of lightning struck him, he suddenly feared she found the DNA test. Holding off sending it in, he waited, hoping if it was true, she would tell him. With a jolt, he ran to the bedroom. Ally, hot on his tail.

"What's wrong?" she asked, but he didn't respond.

Opening the suitcase, relief filled him. The kit sat right where he left it. Whatever made Laney run had nothing to do with the DNA kit.

Ally peered in his bag. "What's that?"

Without thinking, he responded. "A DNA test kit."

Ally gasped, almost choking. "Oh my God, you're Trenton's father. Why didn't I realize it before? You picked her up from dancing naked around the Cupid statue and then you guys...and Trenton came along," she paused and counted on her fingers, "nine months later."

❧

WHEN LANEY ARRIVED HOME, her mother and father were relieved to see her, as Trenton ran to his grandfather and threw his arms around his legs. "Hi, Pops. Did you miss me?"

"A whole bunch," her father replied and she smiled at him, knowing how much the two of them loved each other. Her mother stood by her. "Did Roger find you?"

"Yes, but I don't think he'll be coming around any longer," she said. "Not if he doesn't want me to call the sheriff on him."

"Hrrmph. That young man needed me to take him behind the woodshed. I'd straighten his cheating ass out in no time," Granny replied with a snap.

"Language, Grandmother," Laney reminded the feisty little old lady.

A thump of her cane resounded against the floor. "Maybe so, but the boy should learn it from his great-grandmother rather than some kid at school."

The woman's logic seemed a trifle off, but she liked to keep it in the family.

With a hug, her mother said, "Things happen for the best. Thank goodness you found out now about Roger."

For the last two weeks, Roger had not been the man occupying her mind, but Chase, and he was the only man she dreamed of and worried about. Several times on the way back, her phone rang, but she refused to take the calls.

All the way home, she kept wondering if she was rebounding from Roger, but it didn't feel that way. Actually, it seemed more like a reconnection from so many years ago.

"Pops, do it again," Trenton cried as he lifted the boy up and over his head. This ritual they started when Trenton first learned to walk. Eventually her son would be too heavy for her father to lift over his head, but the two enjoyed the game.

"Your grandmother stayed over from the wedding," she rolled her eyes and Laney smiled.

"That always keeps things interesting," Laney said, watching as her father set Trenton on the ground. He raced over to his grandmother and wrapped his arms around her leg.

"How's my baby?" her mother said, kneeling to wrap her arms around him.

"Not a baby. Big boy," Trenton insisted. "Went fishing."

Suspiciously her mother's brows drew together and suddenly Laney feared what her boy would say about Chase. Everyone believed they were alone and she wasn't.

"You know, I'm tired and should unpack. Plus, I need to get started returning gifts," Laney said, reaching out for Trenton's hand. "And it's movie time."

"Watch race cars with--"

"Come on, son, you haven't gone potty since we came home," she said, interrupting him, her mother's eyes suspicious. The woman had radar that could pick up a fly fart.

Pulling the little boy along with her, she made it up the stairs and safely into the room she shared with Trenton. Why did it seem like she'd run the gauntlet? Now, if only she could somehow return to her calm, ordinary life before a botched wedding and an eventful getaway.

The memory of spending the night in Chase's arms slammed

into her, causing her stomach to tighten with unshed tears as they filled her eyes.

If only she had been honest, but what good would that have done? If she told him, he would have resented her for stealing his dreams. If she didn't tell him, he would resent her for protecting him from the reality of the hand life dealt them. Either way, she was screwed.

An impossible situation, and yet she wouldn't trade it for anything. Glancing at her son, all curled up in bed watching his movie, fighting to keep his eyes open, they would get through this. She would devote her time to raising her boy.

No more men. No more weddings. That pursuit was over. Yet driving back into town, her chest ached, and she felt the need to cry. Really cry, because she loved Chase. But she had to forget him, and hopefully soon, he would move on to his next girlfriend.

After she put Trenton to bed, she went downstairs to visit with her mother and grandmother. Shock rippled through her, leaving her a little uneasy when Ally came around the corner with her dad.

"There she is, the mysterious traveler whose cell phone must be dead or she would realize I've been calling her all afternoon."

"We just got home from the lake not too long ago," she said, her eyes wide with surprise as a trickle of alarm spread through her. Did Chase send Ally here to check on her?

"Funny, I just came from the lake myself. Went to spend the weekend with my friend to cheer her up," she said. "Thought you'd stay at least until tomorrow."

Laney swallowed the rapidly swelling lump in her throat. "Excuse us ladies. We're going to sit outside and catch up."

As soon as they went out back, Ally turned to her. "Why didn't you tell me my brother was at the cabin?"

There were so many reasons why she couldn't talk to Ally about Chase. So many secrets that if she revealed them, Ally would put all the pieces of the puzzle together and be obligated to tell her brother.

"Chase asked me not to say anything," she said. "We barely spoke."

"Really?" Ally said, her eyes narrowing. "I always considered we were better friends."

This couldn't be good. Though, she didn't plan on seeing Chase again, she hated lying to his sister. What did Chase tell Ally?

"By the way, I found your note to Chase," she said.

"Oh," Laney said, stunned.

"Is there anything else you need to tell me about what happened at the lake?" she asked.

Absolutely no way she could tell Ally anything. She just couldn't. Reaching up, her hand landed on her necklace.

"What do you want me to say? This morning, when I woke up I became afraid your brother and I were having a rebound romance. That wouldn't be fair to him, so I came home to try to sort out my emotions."

"Really?" Ally said again, this time with a little more force.

Ally stared at her in a way her friend never had looked at her before. Big brown eyes flashed with anger. As if she recognized Laney lied. Laney could be reacting to Chase on the rebound.

Who was she kidding, she was lying to herself. Always her heart had loved Chase and probably would until she took her last breath.

"Please, Ally, you're my best friend. Sometimes there are things I can't tell anyone about. This is one of those times."

"My brother is disappointed you left without saying good-bye. Maybe the time for running from your feelings for each other has come to an end. Maybe the time has come for the two of you to sit down and talk."

Right now, Laney couldn't deal with Chase. Being with him made her resolve to keep the knowledge of him being Trenton's father weaken. Again, if she told him, he would hate her for keeping Trenton a secret.

No matter what she did, someone was going to be hurt. For both parties, it was best she be the one to bear that pain, because she made the decision when Chase returned to school.

"Later," she told her friend. "Now, I'm too weak to fight him."

Ally stood stiffly. "Call me when you're ready to be honest with me."

Laney watched her walk out the yard and crawl into her car. Could Ally know the truth about Trenton and if she knew, what about Chase? Did he know?

CHAPTER 13

*T*hree days later, she sat eating dinner with her family when someone pounded on the front door. Her father rose and glanced at her. "Are you expecting anyone?"

"No," she said, a nervous tremor radiating from her stomach.

"Laney," she heard Chase yell.

"Chase, Momma, Chase," Trenton said and lifted his booster seat and slid through the railing, his little feet touched the ground and off he went on his short legs, running toward the man he idolized.

"Chase," Trenton cried.

Chase entered the room, she could see the tick in his cheek pulsating, his fists clenched and his eyes crackling with almost hatred. Oh no.

"Hi, buddy," he said, leaning down, trying to change his demeanor but having a tough time.

"Want to play trucks?" her son asked and from the look on Chase's face, he was furious.

"Maybe later," he said to the boy and turned his cold dark eyes on her. "Outside."

Laney's chest tightened, but she led the way to the back yard, hoping her nosey neighbor was not sitting outdoors smoking.

With a resounding thud, she yanked the wooden door closed, to keep prying ears from listening.

Chase reached into his pocket and pulled out a document and handed it to her. Glancing at the papers, she didn't want to see what she already knew, but was unable to stop.

We're pleased to notify you the results of the DNA tests show a ninety-nine percent probability that you are the father.

Oh crap! But when did he take a DNA test?

"How dare you do a DNA test on my son without my knowledge!" she said, raising her eyes and glaring at him. "Isn't that against the law?"

"So sue me," he said. "When I first decided to do the test, I intended to go after the jerk not paying his child support. Imagine my surprise when I learned I'm the jerk who had no clue about my son. How dare you keep the knowledge of his existence from me!"

She took a step closer to him. "Don't you think I tried to tell you, but you were in such a hurry to fulfill your dreams."

"That doesn't mean I wouldn't have listened."

"You didn't call me, you didn't answer my texts, and then when I went over to tell you I'm pregnant, your car was loaded to take you back to school. If you remember, you told me you'd call when you got settled in and you never did. What was I supposed to think?"

The nightmare finally arrived and he reacted exactly how she thought he would. Somehow he would twist this to where it became all her fault. If he'd known, he would have been there for her, like he wasn't there after they came back from the woods. After he went to school.

"Tell me to stop and listen to you."

"Why, when you didn't want to hear me? You were all about becoming a lawyer, so I made the decision to put my life on hold and have my son. We've been just fine without your help," she said.

"You've been doing so fine. That's why you didn't know the man you were marrying was already married?"

"Oh, and your life has been so great? The woman you dated thought monogamy was a board game."

"Then you ran out on me without saying goodbye," he said. "I've called you and you haven't answered my calls."

"Maybe you needed to understand how that feels." Turning her back to him, she walked away, her chest aching, her heart breaking. Not wanting him to see how his words affected her. "It was time to come home."

Everything she feared was now unfolding in front of her and yet she realized he could torture her even worse. Though she still loved him, now he would never forgive her for the secret she kept from him.

He walked up behind her. "Don't think you can run away. I will be very involved in my son's life. He's going to know I'm his father. Today, I filed suit to sue for custody."

Spinning around. "No."

"Now, it's my turn. Since you had him the first three years of his life, I intend to get my share of time with him."

"Don't hurt Trenton to get even with me. He adores you. We can work something out. Just don't hurt him."

Chase turned and strolled away, "Too late. I want my son."

AS SHE WALKED BACK into the house, everyone looked up and stared at her. Glancing around the room, she couldn't find her son.

"Where's Trenton?" she cried, fearful Chase had taken him.

"He's upstairs in bed, watching his movie," her mother said. "A tired little boy didn't need to witness the drama."

"Thanks, Mom," she said and sank down onto the chair, needing to sit to stop her shaking legs.

"The walls in this house are pretty thin and as loud as you two were talking, we overheard who is Trenton's father," her mother said. "Why didn't you tell that young man? He would have married you."

Tonight, she didn't need anyone to berate her for not telling Chase about the pregnancy.

"Because I was a scared twenty-year-old woman who knew about his dream to become a lawyer. A wife and child would have stood in his way. And no way in hell would I abort that baby. So, what was the point?"

Nothing could change. It all happened in the past and no matter what, everyone had to live with her decision. So why not talk about how they would stop him from taking her son away.

"The man deserved to know about his child. All fathers should be there for their children's birth. Chase should be helping you take care of him," her mother scolded. "As his father, he deserves the right to choose whether or not he wanted to see his son, and obviously, he does."

Though she loved her mother, sometimes her advice became too much. When she learned Laney was pregnant, she wanted to demand the father marry her. After Laney declined to tell them who had gotten her with child, she tried to get her to abort the baby. Today she cherished her grandson.

"For four years, you've kept his identity a secret while his boy grew up without a father."

Usually her father stepped in whenever she started on her tirades about Trenton's father. After Chase's dramatic entrance, he went to clean the supper dishes, giving her mother free rein.

"Wait just a minute," her grandmother said.

Oh great, now both of them would gang up on her, voicing their opinions on what she did wrong. Until they walked in her shoes, no one had the right to criticize her decisions. Not even her mother.

"There are secrets in this room that need to be revealed. Don't give Laney such a hard time since her own mother has not been one hundred percent honest," her grandmother said, flashing angry eyes at her mother.

Jerking her head, Laney gazed between the two women. What was she missing here? What was her grandmother prompting her mother to reveal?

"You're one to talk about denying him a chance to get to know his child. Did you ever consider how your daughter will feel learning the truth?"

"Mother, shut up."

Stunned, she stared at the two women, her head spinning. Never in her life had she heard her mother tell her own mother to shut up. Since her childhood, that word had been outlawed in the house.

"What's going on?" Laney asked, knowing she lacked a vital piece of information.

"It's time you told your daughter, Stella," her grandmother said, taking the cane in her hand and bringing it down hard against the floor. "Stop placing your own guilt on Laney. Own up to your feelings. Tell her."

Laney's heart raced in her chest, her blood turning cold. "Mother?"

Her mother shook her head at her mother and then turned to Laney. "When I was in high school, I got pregnant."

"Yes, you told me that's why you and Daddy married," she said, thinking nothing new here. Just old family news.

Taking a deep breath, her mother sighed.

"Your father, the man you adore is not your biological father. After I told Nathan Johnston I was having his baby, he refused to marry me. We have a child together, but he chooses not to claim responsibility for you."

Laney felt as if the floor beneath her feet suddenly tilted.

The man in the kitchen who she called father, who she loved with all her heart and believed from day one to be her father, was not her real father. Unable to stop herself, she started to gag at the realization of the man here in town who had no excuse for not claiming her, was her father, not the man she adored.

With astonishing clarity, she understood she had another family, half-brothers and sisters, aunts and uncles, and even grandparents she'd never met.

"Your father raised you and loved you like his own. You're his daughter, not Nathan's," her mother said.

Just then her father came out of the kitchen. Sensing the tension in the air, he glanced from her mother to her.

"You finally told her," he said. "About time. Just so we're clear, you're my girl, my daughter. Nathan sowed the seeds that created you, but my love for you, along with your mother's, is what made you into the woman you are today. I love you, Laney."

Jumping up, she ran into his arms. "Daddy, I love you, too, and you're my father."

With startling awareness, she realized she would have done this to her son. Queasiness roiled through her stomach, leaving her bewildered. At the moment, she didn't understand how she felt about a man who lived here in town was her biological father and hadn't wanted her.

CHASE WAS positive he would enjoy telling Laney her secret was out, but instead, he felt like Scrooge at Christmas, being obstinate and hurting the woman he loved. Brie, his secretary, tried to warn him, but he refused to listen. Once again, he acted on impulse, wanting to make her experience the pain she caused him with her dishonesty.

Sinking down on the sofa of his hotel room in Cupid, he

asked himself what would make him happy. What would it take to satisfy him? And he knew. Not only did he want the child, but he wanted the mother even more.

Yes, he loved Trenton, not because he was his son, but in the weeks they'd spent together, he'd grown to love the boy. His infectious laughter, his sweet nature that no one had injured yet, his innocence and wonder of the world around him. And especially his love of cars. The kid adored anything to do with trucks and cars.

Missing out on his birth and the first three years of his life saddened him. While Laney had been taking care of their baby and trying to be a full-time student, he could have helped with the burden. The dependability and levelheadedness, he couldn't imagine and wished he had been here to help shoulder some of the responsibility.

Nothing he did today would change the past, but no one would stop him from claiming and seeing his child. Nothing.

Yet, he loved Laney, and in a perfect world, he would have them both. Even if Trenton wasn't in the picture, he would still want Laney. Maybe his younger self had known they would fall in love with one another and the reason he ran all those years ago.

Running so fast and hard from Laney was the very justification for why she never told him about Trenton. Sure, he hurt her. They hurt each other. Her by keeping Trenton a secret and him by keeping her at arm's length so she couldn't tell him she was pregnant.

Pushing his hand through his hair, there were so many questions.

Ally walked through the door of his hotel room. "How did it go?"

"I feel like an ass."

"Oh, it went that well. Didn't I tell you she would not accept you trying to gain custody of Trenton? You're just doing this to make her regret not informing you about your son. The only person you're going to injure is Trenton."

All the old feelings of anger at not knowing about the boy rose inside him.

"I've missed out on the first three years of his life. I'm not missing any more."

"Agreed, but attending law school, would it be conceivable to be here those earlier years? All your life, you dreamed of being a lawyer. So you would have quit school, married Laney, and raised your child?"

A tremor went through him. What a difficult choice. But he believed he loved them both enough that somehow things would have worked out. Yes, he wanted it all, his education and Laney and Trenton. Had Laney made certain he could obtain it all?

"Frankly, brother, I think because she loved you, she sacrificed for your dreams and wisely let you go. No, I don't agree with her decision to withhold telling you, but maybe Laney loved you enough to allow you to do what you needed while she endured a lot."

Ally shook her head. "The rest of us were out partying in college, she sat at home studying, taking classes online and being home with Trenton as much as possible. Don't ever think she didn't put the needs of that child first. Even the night before her disastrous wedding, her thoughts were of Trenton."

Could it be true? Could everything his sister said about her be the truth? Laney mentioned he didn't want to hear her. Didn't she mention he was all about his dreams?

Law school had been a full schedule with no time for anything but cramming. Not a good recipe for a happy marriage and family life.

"There's no doubt Laney is a wonderful mother. In court, I witness women walking all over men to get their needs met. I'm making sure my rights as Trenton's father are recognized by a judge and everyone else."

"Oh, good grief, you obviously don't know Laney Baxter as well as you think you do. The woman would never deny you your rights as his father now that you know. She's not like that."

Though his gut sided with Ally - his head said get it in writing.

"Now, tell me, if you're getting guardianship of Trenton, how are you going to tend to this active little boy?" his sister asked.

That was a problem. Working in downtown Dallas at a firm that required fifty to sixty hours a week, plus, he often traveled to meet with clients. There was no time for raising a child alone, but he had to try.

"There are still kinks to be worked out. I'm sure I will figure something out," he said.

"Chase Hamilton, you're being selfish and I think you want payback. How can you take care of that boy? How self-centered of you to yank him out of his secure environment, take him to the big city and hire a nanny? Put him in the hands of someone he doesn't trust when he's receiving the best right here from his mother?"

Sometimes he despised Ally because she pointed out truthful things to help him realize he was being vindictive. Damn, she was right.

"Do you care anything for Laney?"

Simple question. He loved Laney, longed to make her happy. He wanted to marry her if only she would say the word. Yet, at the moment, she hated him and a court battle couldn't make the situation any better.

"I love her," he said quietly. "I think I have for a long time."

The memory of the two of them lost in the woods that night so long ago came back to him making his chest ache with the knowledge this was the night Trenton was created. He wanted Laney. Had probably always wanted her.

"Well, you're showing it in a strange way. Drop the custody

suit, throw yourself at her feet, tell her you love her and want to spend your life with her."

The idea was tempting, but the attorney in him dismissed the motion to give up on at least sharing custody of his child with Laney.

"I'll take what you've said under advisement. Everyone should understand, I want to see my son on a regular basis. Be in his life, but more than anything, I want Laney."

Today, he wanted it all, Laney, Trenton and the job he enjoyed. But over everything, he wanted his woman and his son. They were most important.

"Then you better do something quick or you're going to lose her forever."

a week later, Laney sat waiting at an outdoor restaurant for Ally to arrive. She'd asked her to lunch and Laney had reluctantly agreed. They'd been friends for a long time and she hated their friendship was now strained due to the court case.

The preliminary hearing was next week and then the actual custody case wouldn't be held for months, her lawyer informed her. Regardless of what any judge said, she would never relinquish Trenton to his attorney father.

Her heart squeezed and she gasped at the sight of her real father. Nathan Johnston sat alone at a table. All these years and she never knew him.

Without thinking, she stood and walked toward his table, needing to say something to him. Standing at his side, he glanced up, his mouth dropping open. "Mr. Johnston, I'm Laney Baxter."

"Yes, I know who you are," he said with a hiss. "Please, go away. My wife and children are completely clueless about you. My oldest son will be here any moment."

A strange sense of calmness came over her. "For myself, I wanted you to understand you may have been the seed that created me, but you're not my father. So there's no need to worry about me telling your family. You're nothing to me."

A pained expression crossed his face as he swallowed hard. "Look, I didn't mean to hurt your mother. We were two kids who got caught. At the time, we weren't even eighteen and I knew I didn't love her. We'd make each other miserable, so I ran."

She nodded, realizing how grateful she felt that her mother never married this man. Sometimes things happened for a reason and her mother never tying herself to this man was lucky for everyone.

"You have the same color eyes as my mother," he said, his voice cracking. "Over the years, I've looked you up and watched you grow into a beautiful young woman. Your mother has done a great job of raising you."

"Yes, my mother and my father made certain I'm loved and taken care of," she said. "My reasons for talking to you today are not to mean you harm or wish you bad karma, I only wanted to meet my biological father. By the way, you have an adorable grandson."

They stared at each other not really knowing what to say, awkward silence stretching between them. Stunned, she realized she had no emotional attachment to this man. Sure, they shared DNA, but that was all.

"A grandson?" he said. "My children aren't married yet."

A look of discomfort, almost a grimace crossed his face. "All these years passed and I should have at least contacted you. Told my family about you and I haven't. Once again, I'm that scared teenage boy who couldn't respond when your mother told me she was pregnant. Please give me some time to tell my wife and children."

Staring at him there were no emotions, nothing. Why had she expected to feel something towards this stranger?

"If you want to leave things as they are, it's okay. My life is blessed and full and we can pretend this conversation never happened. We've both acknowledged one another and I think that's all I needed. Our lives were never meant to be together."

Relief smoothed the wrinkles on his face. "Are you sure?"

"Absolutely," she said. "I'm saying goodbye and we barely said hello. But you've made me appreciate my real father even more."

She turned and walked away just as Ally came into the restaurant courtyard. When she came outside on the patio, Laney sat waiting for her. A newfound tranquility overcame her.

Nathan Johnston would never be her father. Yet, she was glad she had confronted him. And even happier her son would at least know his father and most importantly a relationship with him.

Standing, Ally gave her a hug. "How are you?"

"Good," she said and meant it. The only thing that would make her life better was if Chase told her he loved her. "Ally, I'm sorry I couldn't tell you about Trenton. And I don't expect you to take my side, but I regret not letting Chase know about his son."

Ally nodded. "I'd like for someone to knock some sense into both of you. The two of you are wrong and Trenton is the one who will suffer. No matter what happens, I'm going to bat for my nephew. He deserves a happy life."

THE DAY TO go to court arrived and Laney got up that morning feeling nauseous. The thought of losing Trenton was so frightening. Today, the preliminary hearing where the DNA findings would prove the need for a custody suit. But seeing Chase made her lungs seize.

Facing him again would be tough. Knowing she loved him hurt way worse than anything she'd ever felt before. Even the first time. At twenty, she was young and certain and positive he was meant to go to law school.

Walking into the hall, she saw him standing off to the side

looking at his notes. Turning to her parents, she told them, "Go ahead and go inside. I'll be there in a moment."

Her father touched her arm. "Are you all right? Do you want me to stay here and wait for you?"

"No, I'll be fine. See you inside," she said, thinking how this man cared for her. Yet, would her life have been different if she knew Nathan was her father? Maybe not to Nathan, but to a man like Chase, it made all the difference in the world.

She turned and walked to Chase. "Good morning."

Glancing up, he looked up at her, his brown eyes assessing. "Morning."

"Look, we probably shouldn't be talking before we go in there, but I needed to speak to you. Not to stop the proceedings, but to tell you my feelings before this begins."

"All right," Chase said staring at her suspiciously.

Taking a deep breath, she decided to lay her heart open to him. "When we were young and you rescued me from dancing around the Cupid statue, you were my hero. After getting lost in the woods, you calmed me and said we would be just fine. Confident once the sun came up, we'd find our way back to the car. While we cuddled and tried to stay warm, you slowly gained my trust."

For a moment, she stared at him, trying to help him understand the magnitude of what happened between them.

"That night we created Trenton, and I gave you my heart. We talked about our futures and you told me about your dreams to become a lawyer. Later, when I realized I was pregnant, I wanted to tell you, but your car was loaded, your family stood in the driveway, everyone excited and telling you goodbye. How could I end your dream?"

Chase sighed. "You're right. Looking back, I feared what you would say that day. After that one night, you were the only girl with the ability to keep me from going. At the time, I didn't know about the pregnancy, but if you said stay and be with me, it would have been difficult to leave."

Why had it taken them this long to have this conversation? If only both of them had been open and honest with each since the beginning.

"And I knew that. Somehow, I should have let you know you had a son. Please forgive me, I'm wrong for not telling you. Part of me believed you would return to Cupid, find me, and tell me you'd dreamed of me. Then I would tell you about Trenton, our happy ending would be complete. Yes, it was a silly dream."

Chase took her hand. "No, I often thought of you and wanted to come back."

"Anyway, before we go in here and fight over our son, I want you to understand the time we spent at the lake was wonderful. Yes, I was frustrated and angry when I first arrived, but everything had gone wrong in my life.

"First the horrible attempt at marriage and I still hadn't forgiven you for going to school while I stayed back had a child and went to college online. A part of me always blamed you for deserting me."

"I'm sorry," he said. "I didn't know."

"More than anything, I need to tell you I love you. I've loved you since that night in the woods where you comforted me. In the cabin when you watched Trenton while I was sick, when you protected me from Roger. Since before the night you showed me we're still good together. I love you, Chase, and I understand your reasons for custody. My only hope is that you'll do what's best for our son."

He wrapped his hands around her face, just about to kiss her, when the bailiff opened the door and cleared his throat.

"It's time," he said.

Staring at her, he dropped his hands and they both turned and walked through the wooden door into the courtroom.

❦

THEY WERE BARELY SEATED before the bailiff announced the judge. Of all his cases, this time he'd drawn the strictest, by the book, woman judge. After the official opening of the case, he stood.

"Your honor, may I approach the bench?" he asked.

"Yes, Mr. Hamilton," she said.

Leaning in close so the other party could not hear. "Your honor, things have changed. Please give me some leniency on my actions."

The black robe matched the color of her eyes as she stared at him. "There will be no games in my court, Mr. Hamilton. I'll give you some leniency, but if I think you're acting inappropriately, you'll be fined for contempt. Are we clear?"

"Yes, ma'am," he said.

"Let the games begin," she said softly.

Chase turned and gazed at the family and friends in the courtroom. "When I began the suit to get custody of my son, I'd just learned he was mine. Hurt doesn't describe the emotions I felt since I didn't know sooner. As with all things in life, sometimes we go down roads we never intended to travel and things happen to us."

Pacing the length of the room, he continued. "His mother and I had no intention of creating a baby that night four years ago. Lost together in the woods, things happened we didn't expect. At the time, I realized how very easily I could fall in love with Laney. If I wanted to achieve my goals and dreams, I would need to step away from her, and I did. Not knowing she was carrying my child."

Without looking back, he was certain he was running out of time. "Fate brought us together again and this time, Trenton with her. Slowly I comprehended this boy might be my son. More than anything the fire between his mother and me once again ignited. Only, we were too stupid to see the solution. Even my own sister told me I was being a fool."

Halting in front of Laney, he met her gaze. "Time has a way of making you understand you're being foolish. That maybe I was trying to get revenge on the woman who had kept the truth from me. Does this mean I don't care about Trenton? Oh no, I love that little boy more than I ever imagined."

He paused. "But I love his mother even more."

In the middle of the courtroom, kneeling on one knee with his heart in his throat, he stared at the woman he loved. A huge gasp came from the crowd of family and friends and he feared the judge would slap that contempt charge on him and be hauled off to jail. None of that mattered, this was what he wanted to do.

"Laney, we began our journey by accident, getting lost in the woods. Then we wandered in separate directions. A ruined wedding and a swollen river brought us back together and showed us the love we knew so many years ago still burned brightly within us.

"At this time in our life, I long for us to promise each other forever, give our son the family he deserves, create more children and walk through life side by side. Since that night so long ago, you've had my heart for years. I love you. I double dog dare you to marry me and become my wife."

Tears ran down her face as she walked around the table and took him by the hand and pulled him up to stand next to her.

"I accept your dare." Turning to the honored woman in the black robes, she said, "Judge, would you do us the honor of marrying us right here, right now in your courtroom?"

Chase took her in his arms and kissed her hard on the mouth. "Because I love you so much, I'm willing to wait. Are you sure you don't want a big wedding?"

"And be unlucky again? Oh no, I don't need a fancy ceremony. Here seems the perfect place to start my life with you."

"Let's do it."

She reached up and touched the golden heart necklace she had worn for years.

Suddenly she gasped, her eyes widened and she turned to him. "Did you send me this necklace?"

No longer would he have to hide the grin that spread across his face as he pulled her into his side. "Yes. As I've said, you've had my heart for years."

Kissing her on the lips, love and happiness gripped him. He wanted a lifetime with Laney.

Together they faced the judge, just as the formidable woman wiped tears from her eyes. "Who are your witnesses?"

With a glance, he looked through the group of people. "Her father."

With a smile, she said, "Ally, his sister."

With the two witnesses standing by their side, the judge said the words that joined them as man and wife.

CHAPTER 15

A week later, they stood in his office working with his secretary to change Trenton's birth certificate while their son entertained Brie.

"And then my mommy, she ran around the Cupid statue and Daddy saved her. He rescued her, but then they got lost in the woods together and that's how I was created. Daddy didn't know for a long time that I was born. Now he and Mommy are married and they're going to create me a baby brother or sister."

Laney smiled at her son's story, they agreed there would be no secrets in their family. Trenton knew the truth, but in the simplest explanation without the more intimate details. Still, she never thought he would tell the world about how they came together.

She glanced at Chase, who was working on their wills to make certain if something should ever happen to him, they were taken care of. While on their honeymoon, Chase said he wanted a second baby before Trenton was ready for school. So they were having lots of fun practicing.

"What's this statue he's talking about?" Brie asked.

"In the town of Cupid, there is a superstition that if you dance naked around the God of Love at midnight the first person you see is your true love."

"Worked for us," Chase said, gazing at her. "Only we were a little slow to figure it out."

"It was the summer before my sophomore year in college," Laney admitted.

"The summer before I left for law school."

Brie shook her head. "Look at you. You're married, you have a son, and you're moving to Bride, Texas."

"Yes," Laney said, smiling. After they honeymooned at the cabin, they made the decision they wanted to raise their children in the smaller town. Chase had hired on with a local firm there and she would start teaching in their school district in a week. Everything seem to fall into place for them and they both felt this was the right move.

"Please come visit us anytime," Laney said.

"Visit? I think I'm going to check out Cupid, Texas. After the men I've been dating in Dallas, maybe it's time for me to dance naked around the God of Love and meet my forever love."

After they finished signing the paperwork and Chase had packed up his office, he turned to Brie. "If you decide to run the statue, watch out for the sheriff."

"And the ladies from church. They're trying to remove Cupid from the town square."

"Oh no," she said. "My next time off is not until almost Christmas. Just as soon as I can, I'm going to Cupid."

Chase hugged her. "Goodbye, Brie. Good luck and remember if you ever need a job, you have one in Bride, Texas."

"Thanks, but first Cupid."

Cupid Santa

Brie Simpson glanced around the town square at the boy in a diaper with his arrow drawn back. What was a practical, logical woman like herself doing standing naked in a park waiting for the clock to strike the dancing hour? Never one for crazy stunts, she feared if seized by the law, her friends and family would assume she finally went off the deep end.

Her luck with men was like a bad hand of craps in Vegas. Lucky seven appeared at the wrong time. Sure, this was a superstition. One that could find her looking out between bars.

But the numbers of couples who admitted to having met because of the Cupid Stupid run proved something about this dance brought people together. Enough people, that here she stood in her birthday suit, hoping the man she encountered would accept her plus size body.

The clanging gong struck midnight, the ding dong resounding through the park. Ready to get this process started, she began to jog, shivering in the cold as she chanted the words the legend required you say. "Oh Cupid, find me my true love. Oh Cupid, find me my true love."

According to the superstition you had to make it around the boy in the diaper at least three times, more if you were desperate. At the ripe old age of thirty, even the sixty-year-old janitor in her building looked appealing. Eager to marry and have the family she dreamed of, she was willing to risk it all tonight.

On the third lap, she spotted a figure coming around the statue and sped up.

"Stop," he called. "Halt."

Taking a glance behind her, she detected a man dressed in a Santa suit chasing her and busted out laughing.

"Stop, I'm the law."

"Law? Where's your badge and gun?"

The jolly old man huffed and puffed. Seemed Santa skipped the gym lately.

"Deputy Stephen Austin."

The father of Texas? Sure.

"And I'm Pocahontas. Leave me alone, I'm finding true..."

Stunned, she stopped, staring at the man running toward her. "Oh my, you're my true love. But you're old."

As he ran up to her, he slapped the handcuffs around her wrist.

"I'm your worst nightmare. You're under arrest for public indecency," he said.

His hat fell to the ground and she saw that he wore fake whiskers and his hair was a dark brown.

"Wait, I'm your true love," she said. "No, you can't arrest me."

"Watch me," he said. "Santa is taking you to jail."

"I knew I should have gone to Bride, Texas," she said with a sigh.

Brie's story continues in Cupid Santa

Hopefully you enjoyed Laney and Chase's story. To read an exclusive sneak peek at the next book in the Bride, Texas series please go to http://www.bridetexasseries.com/liz-isaacson/.
Ticket To Bride

Bride, Texas books!
Bride and Prejudice by Bonnie R. Paulson
The Unlucky Bride by Sylvia McDaniel
Ticket to Bride by Liz Isaacson
Bride 'em Cowboy by Twist Roberts
Over My Wed Body by Veronica Blade
Sleigh Bride – by Neve Cottrell
Bride for Hire – Debra Clopton

Thank You For Reading!

Dear Reader,

What a great opportunity to write in a series with these fabulous authors. I'm so honored to be included. Hope you read everyone's story and enjoy Bride, Texas.

As always, if you're inclined, please go to your favorite retailer and let others know what you think. Whether or not you loved the book or hated, it-I'd enjoy your feedback.

If you'd like to learn about my new releases before anyone else, sign up for my New book alerts.. Oh and join my Facebook Readers Group, where there are parties, prizes and fun.

Sincerely,

Sylvia McDaniel

www.SylviaMcDaniel.com
Sylvia@SylviaMcDaniel.com

Determined to find her perfect match, Brie Simpson sets out for Cupid, Texas to test the superstition of dancing naked around the statue and discover true love. Only, to learn destiny betrayed her when she gets handcuffed.

After complaints about the silliness of people dancing naked around the statue, Deputy Stephen Austin doesn't believe in the magic of Cupid with good reason. When he finds himself in a jam, with no one to help plan the annual Christmas party, he's forced to turn to his prisoner.

Can Cupid help a pessimist and a perfectionist come together for the sake of the children and save Christmas?

Nothing says bad judgement like trying to prove a superstition true...

Taylor Braxton, along with a few adventurous girlfriends, decides to test one such superstition on Valentine's Day – the day Taylor's ex-fiancé is to be married. A few bottles of wine help lower her inhibition and go a long way to giving her the courage to try to heal her broken heart. After all, Taylor reasons, what is the worst thing that can happen – the superstition of finding her true love might come true?

Sheriff Ryan Jones is used to getting calls about the odd dancing around the downtown fountain. When you live in Cupid, Texas, there were always some residents who believed if you dance naked around the fountain, you were guaranteed to find your true love. What he doesn't expect is to find the lovely, but spirited Taylor Braxton confronting him at midnight – sans clothing. Unfortunately, a long-held promise and his badge stand between him and what he wants – Taylor.

Will the Cupid Superstition help Taylor and Ryan overcome the past and take a chance on love again? Or will a promise he made to her best friend, and his career, deflect Cupid's arrow?

Also By Sylvia McDaniel
Western Historicals
A Hero's Heart
Second Chance Cowboy
Ethan

American Brides
**Katie: Bride of Virginia

The Burnett Brides Series
The Rancher Takes A Bride
The Outlaw Takes A Bride
The Marshal Takes A Bride
The Christmas Bride
Boxed Set

Lipstick and Lead Series
Desperate
Deadly
Dangerous
Daring
**Determined
Deceived
Defiant
Devious — June 2019
Lipstick and Lead Box Set Books 1-4
**Quinlan's Quest

Mail Order Bride Tales
**A Brother's Betrayal
**Pearl
**Ace's Bride

Scandalous Suffragettes of the West
**Abigail
Bella
Mistletoe Scandal

Southern Historical Romance
A Scarlet Bride
Charity

The Cuvier Women
Wronged
Betrayed
Beguiled
Boxed Set

Contemporary Romance
Return to Cupid, Texas
Cupid Stupid
Cupid Scores
Cupid's Dance
Cupid Help Me!
Cupid Cures
**Cupid's Heart
Cupid Santa
**Cupid Second Chance
Cupid Charmer
Return to Cupid Box Set Books 1-3
Return to Cupid Box Set Books 4-6

Contemporary Romance
My Sister's Boyfriend
The Wanted Bride
The Reluctant Santa
The Relationship Coach

Secrets, Lies, & Online Dating

Bride, Texas Multi-Author Series
**The Unlucky Bride

The Langley Legacy
Collin's Challenge

Short Sexy Reads
Racy Reunions Series
Paying For the Past
Her Christmas Lie
Cupid's Revenge

Science/Fiction Paranormal
The Magic Mirror Series
Touch of Decadence
Touch of Deceit

Want to learn about my new releases before anyone else? Sign up for my New Book Alert and receive a free book.
**Denotes a Sweet Book

USA Today Best-selling author, Sylvia McDaniel is an award-winning author of over fifty western historical romance and contemporary romance novels. Known for her sweet, funny, family-oriented romances, look for her books at all retailers.

Former President of the Dallas Area Romance Authors, a member of the Romance Writers of America®, and Novelists Inc, her novel, A Hero's Heart was a 1996 Golden Heart Finalist. Several other books have placed or won in the San Antonio Romance Authors Contest, LERA Contest, and she was a Golden Network Finalist.

Married for over twenty years to her best friend, they recently moved to western Colorado and are enjoying the mountains. Sylvia loves hiking, camping, knitting and football (Cowboys and Bronco's fan).

www.SylviaMcDaniel.com
Bookbub
The End!